A PARADE AND A PERP

A BEACH HILL COZY MYSTERY BOOK 1

MINA ALLAN

Table
for

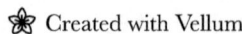

For FJC: this was your idea, too.

CONTENTS

CHAPTER 1

The simultaneous sound of hammering, power tools, and shouting was going to give Andrea Biscotti a headache any second now. She wished she'd tossed earplugs in her bag and picked up another hot chocolate from Didi's before opening the gates at the Rothkin Estate.

"Where does this go, ma'am?" called one of the movers. Raphael, she thought his name was. Raphael's wiry arms were wrapped around one end of an extremely oversized box with MIRROR printed on it. Another mover, Billy, had the other end. Both were red-faced and strained against the heavy load.

"Um…" Andrea consulted her list.

Halfway down the second page, she spotted it: 10 ft mirror, gold—entrance hall.

"Front hall," she said. Luckily, the guys didn't have far to go before depositing it.

As she waited for them to carry in more furniture, or for someone to ask her a question, she took stock of her situation.

Who'd have thought, six months ago—or *one* month ago, for that matter—that she'd be overseeing pop icon Madison Beech's move into her seaside mansion in Beach Hill?

Who'd've thought she'd be overseeing a move, period? Aside from college, she hadn't really moved at all.

And really, who'd've thought that she'd count Madison Beech as a *friend?!*

Andrea had worked with an organizer on Madison's "team" to coordinate the furniture delivery, and Andrea had organized a construction crew to take care of the numerous renovations that Madison wanted on the property that Andrea had grown up calling the Rothkin Estate. The renovations weren't quite finished—they'd done a ton in the four weeks they'd been working—but Madison wanted to be moved in before summer got going and tourists showed up. So far, Madison had kept her move off the paparazzi radar, but, as she'd texted Andrea just last week, the news wouldn't stay quiet for long.

YOU KNOW HOW THE TABLOIDS ARE; she texted in all caps.

No, actually, Andrea didn't know. But she was learning.

Raphael and Billy came in with a bunch of boxes that Andrea sent to the butler's pantry, and the other two movers brought in a hot pink loveseat, wrapped in protective plastic, that Andrea could tell was upholstered in a rich velvet. She checked off each item, sipped her hot chocolate, and resisted the urge to pinch herself.

Andrea was here because Madison had lost a watch, and Andrea found it in Melville the seagull's nest. It was *that* random and that weird. But after a day spent traipsing around Beach Hill, Madison had quickly understood that the people there would leave her alone—or, at least, treat her like a regular—and Andrea had hooked her up with Cordelia Lang, who was selling the Rothkin Estate. After a tour of the property and a whirlwind purchase, Madison had a mansion and Andrea had one of the most popular neighbors in North America.

And Andrea and Claudia had split the sales commission, making both of them very, very happy.

Andrea's phone buzzed.

A video call from Madison.

She opened the app.

"Hey girl!" Madison chirped, her big blue eyes and blond locks filling the screen. Andrea patted her frizz of curls self-consciously. "How's it going?"

Andrea switched the camera view and panned the space. "Loud, busy, and chaotic. Exactly how it's supposed to be."

"Thank you *so much* for doing this," Madison said. Her image spun dizzily as she shifted position and propped the phone in front of her. Madison was draped in a blush-colored smock. A woman in a smartly tailored black dress came into the frame, doing Madison's makeup. "Photo shoot for Gather Magazine," she explained.

"Of course," Andrea said, like she did photo shoots all the time. *The smock must be to protect her outfit.* Andrea glanced at the hot chocolate stain on the front of her shirt.

"It's just so nice to have someone I trust there," Madison continued. "I really appreciate it."

"You still planning on being here for the Boat Parade?" Andrea asked, watching as the woman swiped mascara on Madison's long lashes.

"That's in… ten days?" Madison asked after her stylist was done.

"Yeah," Andrea said.

"Lauri!" Madison called to someone out of camera range. "We're still on schedule for Rhode Island, right?"

Andrea couldn't hear Madison's assistant answer, but she saw Madison nod.

"We are," she said. "I can't wait to relax."

"What about unpacking?" Andrea asked.

Madison laughed. "That team comes in tomorrow. Lauri is going to fly out and supervise."

Oh. Of course.

Andrea clicked the phone off and checked the clipboard. She could take a lesson from Madison's logistics team and do a master to-do list of her own. Aside from overseeing Madison's move in and reno, she had to finish getting the cottages ready for the season.

Andrea's family ran a summer rental business. They owned a dozen cottages on Beach Hill's Point, and had rented them out to summer visitors for nearly five decades. Andrea hadn't intended on taking her business and psychology degree right back to Beach Hill—she intended to go to New York or Boston and work in some glamorous corporate job—but once she realized that in the city her rent and loans would mean she'd be living on saltines, she got her realtor's license and joined the family business.

"That goes in the music room," Andrea said. Raphael carried the stand—was it for a guitar?—down the hall. The high-pitched whine of a table saw added to the cacophony. Andrea rubbed her temples. Something she'd recently discovered about the glamorous life: it took a lot of people to make it work, and she was now one of them.

"Um, excuse me?"

Andrea whirled. The dark-haired guy at the door was not one of the movers, and although she wouldn't have been suspicious of him if he came to *her* door, here she immediately went on alert. Madison did not want the paparazzi getting into the house, under any circumstances. There was someone at the gate, but still. You could never be too sure about these things.

"Can I help you?" she asked icily.

"Um, yeah. I mean, maybe." He went to step over the threshold, into the house.

"Stay right where you are," Andrea ordered. No one was getting dirt on Madison on her watch.

He froze. She crossed the foyer and pointed Billy and Raphael to the master suite, what looked like a giant tufted headboard between them.

She stepped outside the house, onto its grand front portico, and the guy had no choice but to back up, as well. Andrea eyed him: Medium height, dark hair, dark eyes, warm brown skin, Hawaiian shirt, khakis.

"Who are you?" She asked.

"I'm AJ. AJ Garcia," he said with a wide, easy smile. "And who are you?"

"The person who's not letting you in, Mr. Garcia," she said, mimicking her mother's "no-nonsense" tone from when she was growing up. "Now, please state your purpose for being here." She crossed her arms for good measure.

Although outside she was all business, on the inside, Andrea felt a rush of panic. She didn't know how to tell if he was some kind of sleazy paparazzo in disguise, like she saw on TV. And if she screwed up and let someone Madison didn't want in the house, Andrea didn't know what would happen.

AJ—if that was his real name—stood straighter, a playful twinkle in his eye, as though humoring her.

"Madison Beech's tech guru, IT department, and home entertainment wiring guy, reporting for duty," he said in a deep voice. He saluted her.

Ohhhhh… that guy! Madison had told her that her tech guy would be by "at some point" to set up the house. But what if it wasn't actually him? What if he was just pretending to be Madison's tech guy? Anyone could tell that it was moving day at the house—the big truck was visible from the gate even this far from Driftwood Lane.

"Prove it," she said, her eyes narrowed.

AJ ran his hand through his hair, a gesture which, truth be told, Andrea found adorable. Her stomach fluttered. She focused on the matter at hand. "How do I know you're you, and not someone pretending to be you?"

Probably-maybe-AJ stuffed his hands in his pockets. "Well, I don't have a secret code word to give you, but I know that Madison is coming in next week, she wants surround sound through house and I have a blueprint of the whole estate so I can set up the routers and position the relays." He tapped an app on his phone and showed Andrea an email from Lauri, Madison's assistant. "Does that allow me to enter?"

Andrea's cheeks burned. "Um, sure. I think that will suffice," she said stiffly.

"And you are?" AJ asked, one eyebrow raised.

"Andrea. Andrea Biscotti, Madison's friend."

He stuck his hand out to her. "Nice to meet you. And nice to see that you take your gatekeeping seriously." They shook.

And even through her embarrassment, Andrea felt a shock zip up her arm from their clasped hands.

CHAPTER 2

I t took about six hours to get the van unloaded. Andrea marveled at the amount of new stuff that appeared at the door. Over the past month, Madison had gone on a shopping spree. She sent Andrea pictures of some of the new furniture and items that she bought, asking if she thought they would go with her "coastal aesthetic." Andrea answered honestly and tried really hard not to gasp out loud when she saw the prices of the furniture. Madison spent money without even thinking about it—the house had cost over $15 million and she paid for it in cash—but she was also pretty shrewd in her business assessments. Andrea gave her credit. The more she learned about Madison, the more she liked her.

And the more she realized they lived in very different worlds.

Andrea tipped Raphael and the other movers from an envelope of cash that Madison had sent her. She went through all ten rooms of the first floor, looking for AJ, who she finally found in a utility closet in the back hallway.

"Hey," she said to his shirt. He was crouched on the floor, a pile of cables next to him. He stood and his knees popped. Andrea couldn't help it—she winced.

"Occupational hazard," he said. "And hey."

As she stared at his dark eyes and wide grin, she lost track of what she was going to say.

"Oh, ummm… yeah," she flubbed, shaking her head a little to refocus. "So, I'm leaving. I actually have to go to work for part of the day?" She hated that that last part came out sounding like a question. What was *wrong* with her? It wasn't like AJ was the only good-looking guy she'd ever seen in her life. Just a few weeks ago she'd bandaged that construction worker/teacher's hand…Jack. That was his name. *Jack.*

Maybe it was just that she'd seen two good-looking guys in such a short period? She filed that away for later.

"Anyway, I have to leave, and I'm not sure what I should do with… you," she finished lamely. *Get a grip, girl!* she told herself.

"I've gotta finish up here," AJ said. "Lauri and the team need Wi-Fi tomorrow. So, if you want to leave me a key and the alarm code, I can lock up and drop it by your office when I'm done. I promise I won't invite the paparazzi in for a pool party." He held up his hand like he was being sworn to testify on a cop show. "Honest."

Andrea really wanted to trust him. But she didn't want to screw anything up and have Madison mad at her. "Okay. Let me just get back to you on that."

She went into the brand new granite and stainless steel kitchen and texted Madison to see if it was okay that she gave AJ the keys to her kingdom. While she waited for a response, she looked out the windows.

The Rothkin Estate lawn sloped in a green wave from the back of the house to the edge of the bluff. A freshly painted crisp white set of stairs led from the bluff's edge to the beach below, which Andrea couldn't see from her spot. But she could see the ocean sparkling in the mid-May sunshine. A few thin white clouds dotted the sky, and shore birds wheeled above the water. It was a view Andrea had seen her whole life, and never got tired of… *well*, she amended, *this specific view is brand-new to me. But I can definitely get used to it.*

Her phone buzzed. Madison sent her a thumbs-up emoji in response to her questions about AJ. All righty then. He could have the keys to Madison Beech's seaside realm.

Andrea had to go to work.

Andrea had taken her car up to Madison's house, since she had to be there so early, and now she was annoyed that she'd have to find parking on Front Street in the middle of a spring day. Usually, when the weather was nice, she walked or took her scooter, Daisy, to work. She frowned and checked the time as she hopped into her beat-up Honda Civic. Well past lunchtime. Her mood might improve if she ate something.

She pulled out of the estate's drive and hit the button on the garage door opener that swung the gate shut behind her. In spite of her annoyance, she smiled. How many times had she driven, walked her dogs, or scootered past that gate, never knowing what was on the other side? Life was weird.

Front Street wasn't as crowded as she'd feared. She found a metered spot a few doors down from Didi's, outside Andy Li's Beach-tique. She waved at Andy on her way to the cafe.

The door chime tinkled as she went in, and the sweet aromas of cinnamon and cardamom from the ever-present cinnamon rolls reached her nose. Didi's always smelled like heaven. Immediately, Andrea's shoulders relaxed. Coming to Didi's was like coming home--a pink home with a sparkly chandelier and rustic wooden tables.

The lunch rush was over, but the cafe was still busy. Andrea spotted a seat at the counter and slid in.

"Hi, love," Di said. She popped out of the back, wearing her pink checkered "Get the heck out of my kitchen" apron, a spot of flour on her nose. "How'd the move go?" She slid a ham and cheese croissant out of the case and onto a plate.

"Good," Andrea said. Di held up one finger, and took the plate and croissant into the back, where she'd warm it—just like she warmed all of Andrea's pastries, without having to ask.

"Is Beach Hill's most famous resident all moved in?" The

voice at Andrea's back made her jump. Andrea turned and swatted at her cousin Ricky, standing behind her with a cup of coffee.

"Truck's unloaded," Andrea said. "My work there is done."

Di came back with the croissant and slid the plate across the counter, along with a big glass of iced tea. "Fresh this morning," she said.

Andrea bit into the buttery, flaky pastry, with the warm cheese and salty ham, and the stress of the morning melted away.

Or maybe that's my blood sugar improving, she thought.

"Perfect," she mumbled around a mouthful.

"So…?" Didi leaned on the counter, eyes bright and curious.

"Yeah, spill," Ricky said. He'd slid into the empty seat beside Andrea at the counter.

Andrea shrugged. "You know… stuff. Boxes. Furniture for a lot of rooms. It's a big place."

"How's she going to unpack it all?" Di asked. "It'll take all summer."

Andrea swigged the iced tea. "Well, the unpacking team comes tomorrow, so I don't think there'll be much for her to worry about."

"I couldn't let someone unpack my stuff," Di said. "That's too invasive."

Ricky snorted. "Rich people. Must be nice, having other people do everything for you. Pack, move, unpack." He frowned into his coffee cup. "People like me doing all the hard stuff for 'em."

"It's just different," Andrea said. "Celebrities have different responsibilities."

"No real-life ones," Ricky said. He adjusted his Portland Sea Dogs cap.

"Aren't you going to get a new one of those?" Di asked. Ricky grinned and pointed to the rip in the red brim.

"This is my work hat," he said, and put his empty coffee cup on the counter. "You know, actual work? Like hammers and nails, not like ordering things online and having a staff do things for me. And now I've gotta get back to that real-life work with Ratchet Bob," he said with a grandiose flourish. "Because I have to pay my real-life bills!" He did an exaggerated, flouncing walk out of the shop, like he was an aristocratic lord.

"What was that all about?" Di asked.

Andrea watched him leave. "I don't know," she said, eyes on him as he strode down the street, "but it clearly hit a nerve."

Andrea finished her croissant while talking with Di. They agreed that having Madison living in town was going to cause some conversation among the locals.

"I hope people leave her alone," said Di with a sigh. "I mean, most of the people in town are pretty chill, but we get so many tourists in the summer. No one wants busses going up to the estate all day long."

"Well, hopefully that won't happen, but if it does, maybe they'll stop for cinnamon rolls."

Di grinned. "Hmmm. Maybe I should freeze a couple of extra batches of dough in preparation."

"Might not be a bad idea," Andrea said. "Speaking of tourists, we're fully booked for Boat Parade weekend, and Ricky told me that all the slips in the dock are reserved. I'm sure the other rentals are also at capacity."

"Excellent," Di said. "I know it's several days out, but the weather looks gorgeous so far. Let's hope it stays that way."

Andrea raised a pair of crossed fingers, blotted her mouth one last time, and placed her napkin on her plate. She handed Di cash and slid out of her chair.

"And let's hope that the Biscotti Realty voicemail isn't maxed when I get into the office," Andrea said over her shoulder.

CHAPTER 3

The voicemail wasn't quite maxed, but there were a *lot* of messages and even more emails. Andrea was grateful for the croissant's buttery fuel as she powered through them. Most of the calls were from people looking for last-minute rentals before the Boat Parade, and she hated telling people they were too late.

And after the fifth time giving the spiel about Boat Parade Weekend, and why people should book early, she was over that, too.

"The Beach Hill Boat Parade marks the official start of summer in town," she said to the woman who'd wanted a beachfront cottage for the parade weekend—in ten days. "It's been happening for decades. There are a ton of local parties, town wide events, and that's even *before* the parade begins. I have people booking for next year right after this year's parade ends."

The woman on the other end of the phone sniffed. "Well then, I guess I'll take my business elsewhere," she said, and hung up.

Good luck to you, then, Andrea thought.

Andrea rubbed her eyes. Two more calls to make, and one was to Noreen Norris, who back in March had booked

Cottage 10 for a week in August. She'd called in April to confirm, and her latest message also sounded like she wanted more confirmation from Andrea. She cradled her desk phone in her ear to listen again.

"Andrea, dear," came the crisp voice over the speaker. Andrea winced as the woman pronounced her name "AN-DREE-UH", "I wish to discuss the parameters around my August tenth rental with you at your earliest convenience. Please call me back promptly."

Andrea did not want to call her back at all, let alone promptly. But the sooner she got it over with, the sooner it'd be behind her.

She tapped Mrs. Norris's number into the phone, took a deep breath, and plastered a giant, fake smile on her face. She'd read somewhere that faking a smile made you sound friendlier on the phone.

When Mrs. Norris picked up, Andrea said, "Oh, Mrs. Norris, it's Andrea (and made sure to add a little emphasis: "AHN-dRAY-Uh") Biscotti, from Biscotti Realty. You left a message asking for a call back about your August rental. Is there something I can assist you with?"

The fake smile worked, to her own ears, anyway. And to Mrs. Norris's, apparently.

"Hello, dear," the woman's voice responded. "Thank you for getting back to me, although I would have preferred to hear from you this morning." She sniffed, and Andrea rolled her eyes.

"I wanted to confirm my August rental with you, dear. I know things can get overlooked, and I must make sure that my cottage is ready for me upon my arrival."

"Yes, Mrs. Norris," Andrea said through gritted teeth. "I assure you, it will be ready. cottage ten. It's in my book, and the way my system is set up, it is literally *impossible* for me to reserve the same space for two different guests at the same time. Your cottage has your name on it until you leave."

"You never can tell about these things," Mrs. Norris said.

Andrea could picture her: small, gray-haired, fussy-looking, sitting by the phone at home. She pinched the bridge of her nose, fighting to stay pleasant.

"I *can* tell, Mrs. Norris. And as I've said each time we've spoken, two weeks before your rental begins—July 27—I will email you a packet with everything you need to know for your arrival. I'd be happy to send it your way earlier, if that would make you more comfortable?" She used the brightest, happiest voice she could muster.

"Oh, no dear. Totally unnecessary," Mrs. Norris said. "That's a waste of my time. See you in August."

The phone went dead in her hand. Andrea stared at it for a moment.

"The nerve!" she said out loud.

The door chime tinkled, and Andrea quickly replaced the phone receiver and spun in her chair to help the customer.

"Oh, hello," she said. *Oh, hello, indeed.* Jack Townshend was at the door. Weekend construction worker for Mussels for Hire, third grade teacher by day, he had stumbled into her office bleeding and green around the gills a few weeks ago. Since then Andrea'd been trying to work up the nerve to ask him out.

"Are you hurt again?" she teased.

He gave her a grin that would melt chocolate. "Not yet," he said, "but depending on how you answer the next question, I might be."

Andrea's heart kicked into even higher gear. Jack's green eyes didn't leave hers. Andrea waited, hoping he'd say something—anything—soon.

After what seemed like forever, but was likely only a few extra seconds, Jack said, "Would you be interested in going to the pre-parade boat launch tonight?"

Andrea's heart fell into her shoes. "Uh... well, I'd definitely be *interested*," she said, "But I can't. My family is hosting a seventieth birthday party for my uncle, and I kinda need to be there. But—" she said hurriedly, seeing the look in his eyes dim, "I'm totally going to be at the marina, because the party is on the Rusty Nail." The Nail stayed docked in the cove, and it was *the* boat to rent for parties.

What good does that do? She cringed.

"Ah, bummer," he said.

"We could meet for a drink after?" she offered quickly. "I mean, Uncle Eddie is turning seventy, so it's not like he's going to be partying late."

"Perfect," he said.

Jack suggested they meet at the Waverunner, and Andrea agreed.

"Gotta get back to the Scoop," he added, turning to leave.

"Shouldn't you be with a bunch of third graders right now?" Andrea asked, as his hand grasped the knob.

"Uh, school's out for the day."

Oh man. Andrea hadn't even been paying attention to the clock. This day was *flying*.

"Maybe you need a lesson in telling time? I've got some from last week."

Andrea laughed and waved him out. Her day, although long, was looking up. Jack's arrival and invitation were an unexpected boost. Although, oddly, she kept picturing AJ from Madison's house, along with him.

My brain must be on cute guy overload, she thought. She turned to her work—she had a pile of rental agreements for June and July to file and process—and tried to focus. But the paperwork wasn't doing a great job of taking her mind off Jack or AJ.

She shook her head, trying to clear the image of AJ's twinkling eyes.

The bell on the realty office door tinkled, and Andrea shook her head again, because ha-ha, her brain was playing tricks on her. It seemed to think AJ was standing there.

"Andrea?" AJ said. Wait. It *was* AJ! In an instant, it all rushed back: she'd left him the keys to Madison's estate, which he said he'd drop by the office this afternoon. And, voila!

"Hey!" Andrea said. She popped out from behind her

desk, and instantly regretted it, because now she had to stand awkwardly in the middle of the office and didn't know what to do with her hands. "Are you finished already? I didn't expect you so soon!" Her voice sounded high and chirpy to her own ears.

What is wrong with you girl?! Get it together!

AJ chuckled. "I wish. That house is old and I need to get an electrician in there to run some wires for me. Do you have any recommendations?"

"Oh, I sure do!" Andrea responded. She took a breath, then pulled up the names of the three electricians she and Ricky used on the cottages. "Any of these guys should be able to help," she said, writing their numbers on a piece of scrap paper.

AJ thanked her, then stood for a moment, like he wanted to say something else. "I know this is a little forward of me," he said softly, "but um, thanks to this problem it looks like I'm going to be here at least through early next week, and I was wondering if you were around this weekend… you know, to give me all the Beach Hill gossip."

Andrea clamped her lips closed, to ensure her mouth didn't drop open from shock. She hadn't had a date in months, and now two in one weekend? It was an embarrassment of riches.

"I would love to."

"Works for me," AJ said. They settled on the night after next, and a place to meet—the Ocean Front Bar & Grille— and a time. AJ sauntered out of her office, hands in his pockets.

Andrea flopped into her chair. This was shaping up to be the best weekend she had in ages.

CHAPTER 4

Uncle Eddie's party was a blast—the band her cousins had hired played music from the 1950s and 60s, and Andrea delighted in seeing her aunts and uncles jitterbug and twist the night away on the gorgeous party boat docked in the slip. After cake, it was time for her to meet up with Jack.

She got her purse and said some goodbyes, reminding herself to tell Jack that the septuagenarians were still going strong. Her mom found her as she reached the ramp to the dock.

"Heading for your date, Drea?" she asked. Her petite, friendly mom was frequently underestimated by her real estate clients, although Andrea knew better. Francesca Biscotti was one sharp cookie. And when she asked you one question, there was usually something else underneath it.

"Sure am," Andrea responded. "I don't want to be late," she added.

"Keep your eye out for Ricky. I can't believe he didn't show up."

It had been the whispered talk of the night. Andrea's cousin Ricky hadn't made it to Uncle Eddie's party, and everyone noticed his absence. Not only because his big personality lit up any family gathering, but also because Uncle

Eddie was Ricky's father. His three sisters were there, but none of them knew where their brother was—and all of them were annoyed. Andrea was worried. It wasn't like him to blow off a family event. She'd called him, but it went straight to voicemail.

"Will do, Mom," Andrea said. She pecked her mom on the cheek and headed for the dock.

As she crossed the dock, she spotted lights on at another boat, a few slips over. *Season's starting*, she thought. From the Memorial Day weekend boat parade through Labor Day, Beach Hill came to life in a whole new way. Most locals, Andrea included, had mixed feelings about the influx of summer people. And this year, the addition of Madison could bring a whole new type of attention to the small town. *And it'll be my fault*, Andrea thought. But she also believed that Madison would be good for Beach Hill—and, selfishly, Andrea liked having a sliver of access to the popstar's world. And that brought up AJ.

But I'm going to meet Jack.

She shook off the weird feeling as she left the docks, crossed Front Street, and went down a couple of blocks to the Waverunner. On the corner of Front and Sunset, the Waverunner looked like a dive bar from the outside, but it was the locals' best-kept secret.

Andrea pushed the door open into the pub. The gray walls and white trim fit the beach atmosphere without resorting to lobster traps or buoys hanging from the ceiling. She spotted Jack immediately. He was leaning against the bar, arm crooked, holding a pint glass in one hand and giving the bartender, Sammy, his full attention. Sammy said something funny, and Jack threw his head back and laughed. Andrea watched the curve of his throat, the shock of his hair falling back off his forehead. She could hear his laugh from the door of the bar. Butterflies fluttered in her stomach and she smoothed the front of her dress. She also wished she'd touched up her lipstick before getting off the boat. *Sigh*.

Jack caught sight of her and waved her over.

"Hey there, how was the party?" He made space for her at the bar.

"Great!" She told him about Uncle Eddie and Auntie Gee's dance moves and then frowned. "My cousin Ricky didn't show up, though, which is not like him."

"Do you know what he was doing this afternoon?" Jack's brow furrowed in concern. He waved Sammy the bartender over and got Andrea a glass of pinot.

She shook her head. "Working on the cottages, then something with Ratchet Bob. After that, I don't know what. I hope he's okay." She sipped at her drink, suddenly realizing that her mood was a total buzz kill for this date.

"Anyway, I'm sure he'll turn up. How was your day?" she said brightly.

He told her a story about how two of his students drew on their hands to make a Godzilla hand puppets and had a "war." She laughed, especially when he got to the punchline—they'd used permanent marker and were assured of at least two more days of "Godzilla fingers."

Her phone buzzed, and although she normally would never check her texts while out with a cute guy, she was hoping it'd be from Ricky.

"Do you mind?" She gestured to the phone.

"Go for it," Jack said, and he slipped off his stool and headed towards the restrooms.

She flipped the phone over.

What r u doing?

Madison, not Ricky. She typed a quick response—Out, more later—and put the phone face down on the bar.

The longer she thought about it, the more worried she was about her cousin.

But Jack was headed her way, smile wide, and she pushed the family drama right out of her mind.

. . .

For the rest of the evening, Andrea managed not to think about her cousin, but she had a hard time keeping AJ out of her thoughts. *Stop being ridiculous*, she admonished herself. *He lives in California and there's no way anything is happening between us.*

Plus, Jack was no slouch. He had an amiable smile and muscular arms.

"What do you think?" he said.

Andrea hadn't been paying attention at all. "Sorry," she said, cheeks heating. "I guess I'm more tired than I realized. It's been a long day."

Jack regarded her. "I get it. Time to call it a night?"

Andrea nodded and felt miserable while doing so. This was not how things were supposed to go! In a romance novel, Jack would sweep her into his arms, and there'd be a fade to black as he closed the door to her bedroom.

Real life is no romance novel, she thought, grabbing her bag.

"Oh jeez," she said as they stepped outside the bar. She fumbled for her phone.

Jack looked at her with concern. "What's up?"

"My cousin picked me up for the party. I've gotta get a ride," she muttered, searching for the rideshare app.

"I'll drive you," Jack said. "Least I can do. And then maybe we can talk about a do-over some other time."

"Thanks," Andrea said, sticking her phone in the outside pocket of her purse. "That sounds perfect." Inside, she was wondering if he would kiss her, what she should do, should she invite him in—she kind of didn't want to, which was weird, but she was tired and kind of stressed and had to let the dogs out and honestly just wanted to be in her pajamas.

While lost in thought, she followed Jack to his car. Instead of the pickup she expected, he stopped next to a bright orange hybrid SUV. Andrea raised her eyebrows. "Cute!"

He grinned and opened the passenger side door for her. "Thanks. I think ecology is pretty awesome."

Why wasn't she losing her mind over him? *Why* did AJ's face keep popping into her head?

He drove her home, making light conversation, and Andrea slowly felt whatever chemistry she had with him melt away. She liked him enough, but not enough-enough.

"Thanks so much," she said when he pulled into her driveway. "I hate to run, but I have to take my guys for a walk before bed." *Well, that's the lamest end to a date, ever.*

"Of course." He leaned over and gave her a peck on the cheek. "See you around."

As Andrea closed the door behind her, she couldn't help but wonder if she was making a huge mistake.

CHAPTER 5

W hen Andrea entered Didi's through the back door the next morning, she immediately knew something was wrong. Boo, Di's partner, wasn't at the griddle top, for one. The small kitchen was empty, but the front of the shop was packed. Groups huddled around tables, talking in hushed tones. Di had a ginormous platter of cinnamon rolls out, cut into chunks for the taking, on the counter. Boo stood at the end of the counter, topping off the already-full sugar and maple syrup containers, eyes out the window.

"I was so distracted, I left the cardamom out of them," she said apologetically to anyone who approached the tray. "They're just regular and I'm giving them away; I don't know what else to do."

"What's going on?" Andrea said. She grabbed a gooey hunk of cinnamon roll. Cardamom or no cardamom, they were delicious.

"You didn't hear?" Di's expression was shocked. "It's all anyone's talking about."

"I left my phone in Jack's car last night," Andrea said, wincing at the thought of the terrible impression she'd left. "What?"

Didi let that piece of gossip go, which is how Andrea knew

whatever it was must be serious, and pointed at the front of the shop. "Look."

Andrea went to the plate-glass window. Front Street Park and the statue of Gilbert Rothkin were where they always were, but as she turned her head a little towards the docks…

"Oh no." Her mouth went dry, seeing the police cars, crime tape and people in uniform all over the beachfront. "What happened?"

She expected to hear that someone's boat had been broken into or vandalized. Although infrequent, it did happen. Teenagers, mostly, looking for a good time or to cause trouble. But ever since motion sensor cameras had gotten popular and inexpensive, that happened less and less often.

"They found a body," Didi said. "In the cove, next to one of the boats."

"What? Someone drowned?" Living in a seaside community, you heard the occasional story of some inexperienced swimmer getting pulled into a riptide, or a drunken boating accident. But that was even more rare than the dockside break-ins.

"Maybe?" Didi said. She lowered her voice. "Two of the officers came in to grab coffee—I sent out the catering urn so they don't need to keep coming for refills—and I heard one say that it *wasn't* an accident."

"Murder?" Andrea's voice was too loud for the quiet tea shop, and several heads turned in her direction.

"Shhhhh!" Didi said. "I don't want to get my source in trouble or spread wild rumors."

Andrea nodded and went back to the counter. She absently grabbed another hunk of sliced cinnamon roll while Di fired up the steamed milk machine for her hot chocolate.

Who could the victim be? She remembered the lights on that other boat. Was it someone on there? Or what if it was someone she knew? Andrea's stomach clenched uneasily at the thought, but her curiosity kept pushing her down an uncomfortable road.

She'd been on the docks the night before, for Uncle Eddie's party. Was it someone she'd seen? Oh goodness, she couldn't imagine it was someone at her uncle's party, but what if? How could she get more information? Stupid phone in Jack's car.

Di handed her her hot chocolate, and Andrea had an idea.

"Hey, would you mind if I take these over to… you know," she gestured with a nod towards the window and the police activity beyond. "I bet they're hungry."

"Go for it," Didi said. She slid a couple more rolls on the tray and sliced them quickly, so it was full again. "I have at least a half dozen more I can keep on the counter here. Bring back the tray and some good info."

Andrea slid an arm under the tray, waitress-style, and with her hot chocolate in one hand and a bounty of rolls in the other, headed for the door.

The air was damp and cool, with a little bit of fog over the cove. The docked boats bobbed gently in the water, and if you didn't look a half block north, you'd never know something was wrong.

What am I doing? Andrea thought as she crossed the street and stepped into the park. She decided not to question herself, and just beelined for a group of uniformed police officers standing near Didi's coffee urn. No one called out to her, and as she got closer, she felt less self-conscious. She was bringing pastries, after all. And everyone loved pastries. Especially if Didi made them.

"From Didi's Tea Shoppe," she said to the knot of officers, setting the rolls down on the hood of the car next to the coffee urn.

A young female officer turned to her. "Thanks," she said gratefully. "I've been here since five and I'm starving." She helped herself to a roll, and a couple of others did, too.

"What a morning," Andrea said, hoping it would be an opening for someone to immediately tell her what happened.

"You're not kidding," said the young officer. Another person in uniform spun around, and Andrea's heart sank. Niles Needermeyer—Niles the Nosepicker, as he was known in her second-grade class, puffed out his chest and glared at her.

"This is an active investigation," he said. "No one here is sharing any details with looky-loos. Right, Riley?" The younger cop flushed.

"Oh, hey Niles. I don't want to get anyone in trouble," Andrea said. "It's just…" she gestured broadly with her arm, and forgot it was the one holding the hot chocolate, which sloshed out of the cup and splashed her hand, "it's obvious that there's some stuff going on, you know?" She grabbed a napkin to mop up her wrist and the cuff of her shirt, wincing at the heat, but glad to have something to do.

"Thanks for the rolls," Riley, the young officer, said. A few others nodded and mumbled the same through stuffed cheeks. The platter was nearly empty.

Niles' belt radio crackled, and before he stepped away, Andrea heard, "Patrol group to slip 24."

That must be where the body came from, she thought. Several uniformed officers thumped across the wooden docks, towards the boat she'd seen illuminated the night before.

Andrea brought the tray back to Didi and gave a hard shake of her head to Di's raised eyebrow. She didn't have enough information to share yet, but she had an idea as to how to get more.

She scooted out the back door of Didi's shop, cut through the alley, and went up the stairs to the parking lot above Front Street. From there, she had a view of the entire Beach Hill coastline.

Shaped like a wide U, Beach Hill's coast made for a sheltered cove for boats. Her family's cottages stretched towards the

Point, on the left, with the carousel and the end of Front Street Park at the bottom left of the U. The dock and slips were in the middle, dotting the water. To the right was the rest of Front Street Park, and as the coast turned out towards the water, over-sized homes with incredible views nestled into the shore. Behind her, where Front Street met Driftwood, was the Rothkin Estate.

A crowd gathered on the docks. Police tape criss-crossed the scene and blue uniformed bodies went back and forth along the wooden path. There was a lot of activity on a large pleasure boat… or would it be a small yacht?… white, trimmed in beautiful dark wood with crimson sails. The Master Peace. She'd noticed it leaving Uncle Eddie's party the night before, strung with twinkling lights.

A chill ran down her spine. Had she been looking at a dead person's boat while celebrating her uncle? When had they died?

A police officer turned to the radio clipped to his shoulder. A moment later, two other uniformed officers emerged from the throng, gathered around the coffee urn and jogged across the park and to the slip. They conversed, then adjusted their belts, walked back across the park, got in a marked car, and drove away.

Hmmmm… Andrea thought. Someone had clearly sent the two on an errand of some sort. Looking for suspects?

A flash caught her eye. It came from the boat.

It came again.

Photos. Someone was using a flash camera inside the boat. A few more flashes, then she spied the photographer coming to the deck. She snapped several around the perimeter of the vessel, then spent a long time taking shots over the starboard side.

A car pulled in to the lot, kicking up gravel and startling her. She stepped aside, frowning.

On TV, cops took pictures at murder scenes. It was looking more and more likely that someone had been killed. Was there a body on the boat? Or was Didi right, and it was in the water?

Things like this just didn't happen in Beach Hill.

She made her way down the stairs, back to Didi's to fill in her friend. A lot of things were happening in Beach Hill that hadn't before.

CHAPTER 6

After reporting what little she knew to Di, Andrea went home, clipped Amaretto and Limoncello's leashes to their collars, grabbed some "business bags," and headed out. She needed to get her phone back from Jack, but she'd never bothered getting a landline, so had no way to reach him. So, of course, she went back to Didi's. She tied the dogs to the "Pup Parking" hitch outside, and they promptly curled up in a warm patch of sunshine. It was still busy, but the crowd had changed. Andrea spotted Capt. Mike Rimbeau, from the Slip Shack, deep in conversation with her cousin Ricky. She wondered if the police had talked to Mike this morning, since he monitored all the boats in the cove. And she *really* wanted to find out why her cousin hadn't come to the party. If it was any other excuse than "kidnapped by aliens," Andrea didn't want to hear it.

"What's up?" Didi said, taking her attention away from the two men and passing her another small hot chocolate—the second of the day. She was at her limit.

"Figuring out my life," she said. "But hold on, I want to talk to Ricky—" however, when she turned to the table where he and Mike had been sitting, it was empty.

After giving Didi all the details about what she saw at the

waterfront, then the scoop about her lackluster date, she held her hands out. "*Now* what am I supposed to do?"

Di wiped some crumbs from the counter into her cupped palm. "First, you're going to get your phone back from Jack, then you're going to go on that date with AJ tomorrow night. Then see where you're at."

Andrea grinned. "You're the best."

Didi handed her two peanut butter dog bone-shaped cookies. "You're right. Now go and let me know what happens."

Andrea waved on the way out the door. Lemon and Amaretto were all wagging tails and pleading eyes when they saw—or smelled—the treats in her hand.

"Here you go, boys," she said, passing them their biscuits. While they gobbled, Andrea untied their leashes and plotted her next move. The Mussels for Hire work van was parked outside the Sip 'n Scoop, so she thought she'd start there and see if Jack was around.

As she and the dogs maneuvered down Front Street, she popped her head into a couple of shops along the way, saying hi to Andy Li and a few other shop owners.

Not that I'm stalling or anything, she thought. The closer they got to the Sip 'n Scoop, the clammier her hands became. Things had been so awkward with Jack last night… how would it go today? Did he think she left her phone in his car on purpose? And, on the other hand, would he think she was so super flaky that she'd forgotten it? The dogs' leash slipped across her palm like it was greased.

Gross.

They were in front of the Scoop. The dogs sniffed at the door. She inhaled and exhaled to the count of four, trying to steady herself. The ice cream shack was oddly quiet—no sounds of saws or nail guns. She knocked.

No response. She knocked again. The dogs whined.

"Chill out, guys. We're going to the beach in a few."

Where was the crew?

She stood there for a moment more, then, just as she was going to let herself in to the ice cream store, a muffled thump came from the rear of the building. She and the dogs walked around the shop.

Behind the Sip 'n Scoop was a mess: piles of lumber, some folding tables stacked on a dolly, crates and assorted construction equipment… and Jack. Wearing noise canceling headphones.

"Hey!" Andrea called. "Hey, Jack!"

His back was to her. He rummaged through a crate at his feet. After admiring the view, Andrea didn't know what to do. Should she tap him on the shoulder? Wait until he turned around? Yell louder?

She didn't have to decide. Amaretto and Limoncello, clearly sick of waiting and excited to see a friend, jerked forward and their leash slipped right out of her sweaty palm. The dogs bounded over to Jack, who jumped when they accosted him with wags and licks.

"Hey there!" he said to the dogs. "Easy!"

"Boys! Come!" Andrea called. The dogs obediently trotted to her, and Jack turned around.

"I thought they were yours," he said. He hung the noise-cancelling headphones around his neck.

"Yeah, they're mine. They helped me sniff you out this morning," she said, hoping he'd appreciate the joke.

Jack grinned, lighting up his features. "Nice. Looking for ice cream? Should be open next week."

Andrea shook her head. "Looking for my phone. I think I left it in your car last night, and, uhhh, I couldn't call you to check."

"Guess not, huh? So, the bad news is I don't have my car down here. One of the guys picked me up this morning. I can look when I get home this afternoon and drop it off or something?"

Andrea's heart gave a twinge. Had the date been so bad that he didn't even want to see her again to return her phone?

"Sure," she said. "That would be great. You can even leave it at the office, since that's where I'm going today."

"Perfect. I have to swing by my mom's later."

Was the flood of relief she felt out of proportion to his statement? Probably.

"Okay then. Thanks for a great night last night," she said brightly.

"Was it great?" he asked, eyebrow raised.

Andrea's face flamed. She gave a nervous laugh. "Okay, you're right. I was… distracted. So no, it probably wasn't great."

Jack smiled, hair flopping in his eyes. "We can try again?"

"Let's."

The rest of Andrea's day was normal. Since she didn't have to go to Madison's, she spent it in the Biscotti realty office, neck-deep in paperwork. The Bunco family was coming in early—the cottages didn't officially open until Friday, but they'd insisted on a midweek arrival—and that meant readjusting the linens delivery and making sure she had cleaners lined up.

She also had time to run to the bank and get a couple of "just-in-case" gift cards to Didi's—sometimes renters got grouchy about one thing or another, and a cinnamon roll could usually smooth over any issues. When she came back from Di's, she found a bag hanging from the Biscotti Realty doorknob, her phone inside, along with a sticky note decorated with a smiley face.

Was that relief from not having to run into Jack again, or from getting her phone back? Hard to tell.

Regardless, she felt good about her accomplishments. At home she had an early dinner, found the silliest monster movie she could, curled up with the boys on her bed, and watched it until she fell asleep.

CHAPTER 7

The tiny cabin shook with pounding thuds. There was a dinosaur outside, but Andrea was afraid to look out the window. She hid under a table, covering her head as the blows got louder. Any second, she knew Godzilla would squash her—

She woke with a start. The pounding came again—but from her front door, not Godzilla. Limoncello and Amaretto were barking like crazy. How long had this been going on?

"Drea!" came a muffled female voice. "Wake up!"

She shot out of bed. *Am I late for work? Is Mom okay?*

"Coming!" she yelled. Her hands shook with adrenaline. She grabbed a pair of yoga pants and threw a sweatshirt over the concert tee she wore to bed. The dogs ran to her, then back to the front door.

"Shhhh!!!" she chided them.

As she raced into the front room of the apartment, she glanced at the clock on her microwave: 5:42am.

What?!?

No wonder she felt so disoriented—and now she was terrified.

"Who's there?" she had the presence of mind to call out, before throwing the door open.

"It's Gwen. Open up!" she barely recognized her cousin's

voice, and when she opened the door, she barely recognized Gwen.

The two nights before, she'd seen Gwen at the party for her dad, Uncle Eddie, dancing and singing, wearing a green dress with a skirt that flared out as she spun, red hair piled high.

Now she was in a ripped t-shirt, a pair of plaid pajama pants, her hair was a tangled mess, and there were mascara streaks on her cheeks.

"Gwennie! Oh my goodness! What happened?!" Andrea pulled her cousin into the apartment, sat her on the couch, and wrapped her in a blanket. The dogs immediately settled on either side of her cousin, offering comfort. Gwen promptly burst into tears.

"It's Ricky!" she wailed. "The body they found in the slip yesterday morning? They think it was *him*." Gwen couldn't continue. Sobs shook her shoulders.

Andrea couldn't process what Gwen meant. They thought Ricky was the body? That didn't make sense—she'd seen him yesterday. That meant—

oh.

Oh.

Oh, no. That meant someone—the police, most likely, thought Ricky was the *killer*.

CHAPTER 8

I t took several minutes, but Andrea cooed and comforted Gwennie until her sobs subsided to sniffles. Then she poured some kibble in the dogs' bowls, dug out her coffee pot, skimmed the directions, and made what she hoped was extra strong coffee. While that was percolating, she whipped up some instant hot chocolate mix for herself, splashed some water on her face, squared her shoulders and sat down next to her cousin. A million questions zinged through her mind:

Why was Ricky a suspect? What had he done to make the police think that he'd committed the crime? For that matter, was he actually a suspect, or was Gwennie upset because of something she'd heard? Had anyone actually spoken to Ricky?

The list went on and on. Andrea thought back to every episode of every cop show she'd ever watched. She couldn't push Gwen, because she'd never get information out of her— no matter how badly she wanted to know the answers to these questions, she had to approach things gently.

The coffee pot beeped, and Andrea poured a mug for her cousin. She grabbed a tray, stuck some milk and sugar on it, and scrambled through her mostly empty cabinets for something sweet to include.

Graham crackers would have to do.

She carried the loaded tray to her living room and put it on the coffee table. Gwen was still wrapped in the blanket, staring off into space, exhaustion covering her features. Limoncello was curled in her lap, and she absently stroked his head.

"Gwennie? Hon?" Andrea spoke softly. She sat across from her cousin in an overstuffed denim chair, Amaretto snoozing on the ottoman at her feet.

Her cousin blinked and shook her head, as though she didn't remember where she was.

"Oh. Thanks, Drea." She poured milk into her mug and added sugar, stirring it for a while.

"Do you want to start at the beginning?" Andrea said, tucking her legs under her.

Gwen wrapped both hands around her cup and stayed silent long enough that Andrea wondered if she'd heard her.

"It happened really fast," Gwennie began. "But not, you know? We were all so mad that Ricky didn't show up for Dad's party. After it was over, I dropped my dad off at home and was going to meet my friend at the Waverunner for last call. I'd just pulled out of Dad's driveway and my phone binged with the tone it's set with for texts from Ricky. I'd spent so much time being mad at him that night, but had finally gotten over it and had a good time during the second half of the party. I didn't even want to read it and ruin the other half of my night, you know?" Gwennie's face was beseeching.

Andrea nodded. She understood what she meant, for sure.

Gwen stared into her coffee cup. "So I didn't check it," she said softly. "It was probably the dumbest thing I've ever done in my life." Her lip trembled, and Andrea saw another emotional storm headed her way.

"Did you delete it?" she asked quickly.

Gwen shook her head, then took out her phone and put it on the coffee table.

"It's here," she said. She let the blanket fall to her shoulders and stood. "You read it." She turned and headed down the hall towards Andrea's bathroom.

Andrea waited until she heard the door close before she reached out and grabbed the phone. Gwennie hadn't locked it. She tapped the messages and there was Ricky's name.

She opened it.

Hey, we need to meet Behind Sip n Scoop in 30 everythings wrong

Andrea looked at the screen of her cousin's phone, as though it would hold some answers. What was wrong? What had he wanted? Maybe he'd seen something? She tried not to be frustrated at Gwen, but she wished she had read the text and gone to see what her brother wanted.

Gwen came back from the bathroom. She'd scrubbed the makeup off her face and unpinned her hair, so although she still looked exhausted, she wasn't as disheveled.

"Can you help, Drea?" she asked, her blue eyes beseeching. "Please?"

Andrea furrowed her brow. "I'm not sure what I can do, Gwen," she said. "Have the police contacted you?" Limoncello whined at the door. The dogs needed to go out; their morning routine was shot.

"Contacted me?! They *took him*. They're holding him."

"What?" Andrea was sure she hadn't heard right. "What do you mean, the police have him'? Like, he's at the station?"

Her cousin nodded. "Yes! That's what I've been trying to tell you. You need to help him!"

"Help him? I don't know what to do."

"You know everyone downtown. You can find out what he meant by this," Gwennie said. "Just ask some questions. He does so much work for you. Do you really think he'd hurt someone?" At this, her voice had an edge of anger.

Andrea sighed and grabbed the leashes. She understood what Gwennie wanted her to do, and part of her—the insatiably curious part—was kind of excited by the prospect. Maybe she *could* help?

"I'll try," she told her cousin, hand on the doorknob. Amaretto wagged his tail and sat obediently for it to be clipped on his collar. "But look, I need you to understand that there isn't much I can do—I'm not a lawyer or a police officer, obviously—but I'll ask around and see what I can find out."

Gwen threw her arms around Andrea in a hug so tight it made her gasp.

"I knew you'd be there for us," she said into Andrea's neck.

Andrea hoped that whatever she found would be what Gwennie—and Ricky—wanted to hear.

Andrea took the dogs out for a potty break, then came back in and tried to get more information out of Gwen, but her cousin didn't have anything to add except more guilt over not reading the text. When Gwen left, it was close to seven. Andrea rubbed her eyes, which felt gritty with exhaustion, and took a long, hot shower. After she was dressed, she searched for a notebook, hoping that jotting notes could help her make sense of things. Unfortunately, the only one she could find was one with a giant, rainbow-sparkle unicorn head on the front, with the words "Sparkle wherever you go" printed above it in bright pink. Clearly, one of her nieces had left it behind.

So professional. Andrea laughed to herself. *Well, even Nancy Drew had to start somewhere.* She decided to lean into it and found a purple pen, then curled up on the couch with the dogs, who promptly went back to sleep. She set a fifteen-minute timer on her phone and made a list.

What I know
Someone was murdered
The body found near a boat with red sails
Slip 24
Ricky is a suspect
He missed Uncle Eddie's party
He texted Gwen. She never met him
Ricky worked on the cottages during the day
I saw him at Didi's yesterday AM

She tapped the top of the pen against her leg. There was something on the periphery of her thoughts, but she couldn't quite remember. *Wait!* Hastily, she added,

Ricky helped Ratchet Bob in the afternoon

To her list.

Okay, she thought. *Two things I can do: Talk with Ratchet Bob and find out more about Slip 24.* She wasn't sure that it would help Ricky, but it would at least give her something to tell Gwen. And she could still get it done as she prepped for Boat Parade weekend.

She hooked Limoncello and Amaretto's collars to their leashes, taking them out for another morning walk.

"We've got work to do, boys," she said as she went out the door.

She let the dogs lead her down the steps of her apartment, which was attached to the back of a rambling beachside retreat owned by Mrs. Dalyride, Andrea's former sixth-grade teacher. Even now, as an adult, Andrea still didn't know Mrs. D's first name—and she was pretty sure the retired teacher preferred it that way.

The plus side of living here was that the rent was cheap and the apartment big, she could have the boys with her, and Mrs. D traveled quite a bit and so the main house was frequently empty. The downside was when Mrs. D *was* home, she'd often invite herself in for tea and an examination of Andrea's business.

Luckily, Mrs. D was out of town, and Andrea, Amaretto, and Limoncello strode right down the driveway, turned onto Driftwood Terrace, and motored toward the beach.

While the dogs sniffed and did their business, Andrea let her mind turn over what little she knew about the crime and Ricky's potential involvement. The first piece of info that she needed was to find out who, exactly, was killed. She was beginning to think that it was someone from out of town, as there had been no gossip through the Beach Hill grapevine about anyone missing or dead.

If it *was* an out-of-towner, that made things both hard and easy. On the one hand, Ricky was a total local who rarely had opportunity or interest to hang out with non-Beach Hill friends. *Did he even have non-Beach Hill friends?* Andrea wondered as she bagged Amaretto's business.

There was also the issue of her own involvement. Who was she to go snooping around in someone's potential murder?! Sure, she loved solving puzzles and was definitely interested in what was going on, but she was hardly a detective.

But that could be a good thing, her brain answered. She might actually be able to see patterns the police missed.

They'd reached the water, and, predictably, Limoncello lunged toward the lapping waves while Amaretto hung back. Andrea followed Front Street Park to the Point on the shoreline path, Limoncello whining and straining the entire time. When they were far enough from the parking lot, Andrea unclipped Lemon's leash. The little dog dashed into the surf, not caring that the water was likely freezing. Amaretto plunked his butt in the sand and watched his buddy, just like he did every morning.

Andrea inhaled the salty tang of the air, then studied the slips and the dock. The police were still there, although not as many as before. The yellow crime scene tape perimeter was smaller, too. She also spotted crime tape around one of the slips—number 24, presumably—and the boat that was moored there: The Master Peace. Its red sails made it stand out from the other boats. Not the biggest boat in the cove by a long shot, but not a dinghy. She recognized it, but didn't know who it belonged to.

As she watched, a couple of uniformed police officers walked around, patrolling the scene—not collecting evidence, but keeping people from getting close to the crime scenes. She wondered if they would tow the boat somewhere.

Amaretto broke out into a bark, startling her. The dog trotted to the water's edge, yapping and bouncing with excitement. Andrea followed his gaze. Limoncello was in the surf, further from shore than where he usually explored. The ocean around him was frothy, as if he'd been diving. His little head was all but obscured by something he was bringing back to the beach.

Did she need to rescue him? Andrea's heart stuttered in her chest. But a moment later, Lemon had all four paws on the sand, something dark and dripping wet clenched in his teeth. Amaretto beat her to him, his tail wagging proudly as if to say, "Look at what my brother did!"

Andrea knelt next to Limoncello, who dropped the item right in front of her. "Good boy, Lemon!" she said automatically.

It was a baseball hat.

A Portland Sea Dogs hat with a red brim and a tear across the front.

Ricky's hat.

Andrea's whole body froze like the time she was foolish enough to partake in the Polar Plunge on New Year's Day. She couldn't even think: Her mind went blank.

Then Limoncello barked once, sharply, as if to alert her. She snapped back to herself, first staring down at the baseball cap in the sand, then looking to see what caught Lemon's attention.

Someone was coming. Someone in a blue uniform.

Andrea had to act fast. Should she show the cap to the police? She hated these sorts of decisions.

Not that she'd ever had to make ones like this before.

She grabbed the cap and held it casually—or as casually as she could, knowing that there was a police officer headed her way.

She directed her focus back to the dogs, clipped Lemon to his leash. "What's up, buddy?" she said as normally as possible to Amaretto, who was sitting at her feet, staring up at her, long tail frowsing across the sand.

"Hey there!" called the cop. Andrea turned to her, pretending—not having to try too hard—to be startled.

"Oh, hi!" As Andrea got closer, she realized it was the young female officer, Riley, the one who really liked the cinnamon rolls. "Is there a problem, officer?"

"No, ma'am," she said. "I just wanted to let you know that we'll be closing The Point shortly."

"Why?" Andrea found that if she asked a question and just waited, eventually people responded

The officer looked uncomfortable, like she wasn't sure how much she was supposed to reveal.

"Well, umm… the dive team is coming in, and they're going to launch from the beach."

"The dive team?" Andrea repeated, and waited. *Please don't notice the hat… please don't notice the hat, she kept repeating in her head.*

The officer looked at the sand. A larger wave came in and the dogs dodged the spray. "They're looking for… stuff," she said lamely.

Andrea clutched the wet hat tightly in her left hand. *I bet,* she thought.

"Okay," she said brightly. "We're about done with our stroll, anyway. Aren't we, boys?" She directed to the dogs, who obligingly shook the wet sand off their coats. "Good luck with… whatever you're looking for," she told the officer.

"Thanks," the officer replied. "Go Sea Dogs," she added.

Andrea didn't respond, just fought the urge to panic, forced a smile, and lead the dogs back toward Front Street Park.

It wasn't until her feet hit the sidewalk across from Didi's that she allowed herself to think about what she'd done: Walked away from a police officer in an active investigation, holding a (likely) piece of evidence. She watched enough cop shows to know that this was a Very Bad Idea.

No matter what she *thought* she was going to tell Gwen, she'd just involved herself in a murder mystery.

CHAPTER 9

S he dropped the boys off at her office. Both trotted over to
their plaid beds behind her desk and curled up, ready for
a nap after their early morning. She took Ricky's hat and put
it in a plastic grocery store bag, sure that she would spend
most of the rest of her life in jail just for hanging onto it.

I can always turn it in later, she thought, *if it seems necessary. I
walk the dogs on the beach every morning. Lemon could have picked it up
at any time.*

The thought was cold comfort, but she pushed it aside
while she refreshed the dogs' water and told them to be good.
They barely opened an eye when she left the office and
headed to Didi's.

Murder is good for business, she observed wryly. Di's was
packed yet again, and she had to wait in line for her hot
chocolate. People crammed the window seats, pretending to
drink their coffee but really peering across the street.

"Dive team's coming in," she told Di in lieu of good
morning.

Di raised an eyebrow. "And you know this how?"

"I ran into Officer Helpful while walking the boys," she
said.

"There's the dive boat!" A woman at the window called.

Di nodded and slid Andrea's hot chocolate across the counter. "You look beat. Rough night?"

Andrea glanced around the shop before answering, making sure everyone was focused on what was happening across the street. She lowered her voice and quickly filled Didi in on Gwennie's visit, ending with Gwen imploring her to help Ricky.

"Are you going to?" Didi asked, expertly slipping a cardamom cinnamon roll off her spatula and onto a pewter plate. She handed the plate to Andrea. "On the house. You need a boost after this morning."

Andrea smiled gratefully and, to buy time before answering, took a bite of the sticky goodness, letting the warmth spread through her body.

"I think I am," she said. "Although I'm not sure what I can do yet."

A customer came to the counter. "You'll figure something out," Didi said as she moved to help the gentleman. "I believe in you."

Andrea thought about the hat wrapped in its bag in her office.

She'd better figure something out, fast.

She spotted Ratchet Bob through the tea shoppe window before she'd even finished her hot chocolate. Taking a last sip, and wiping a dot of whipped cream from her nose, she waved at Boo when he poked his head out from the kitchen. Andrea skedaddled out of the store.

Ratchet Bob was pushing a rusty lawnmower up Front Street, likely taking it home.

"Hey, Bob!" Andrea called.

He stopped and turned, waiting for her.

That's when Andrea realized she didn't actually know what she was going to say. TV detectives made this sort of stuff look easy, but she didn't have a team of writers handing her a script. Not to mention the fact that Ratchet Bob was not the most sociable person in Beach Hill.

"Yeah?" he said, when she got closer. "Whaddaya want?"

He was wearing his typical grimy blue coveralls, embroidered with his name in red, over the left pocket. He was the local fix-it guy for anything with an engine—especially lawnmowers and outboard motors.

As far as Andrea knew, he'd never been married and always lived in a tiny house at the end of Sand Dollar Lane. The house was so small it could have been featured on one of those trendy home design shows, but there was not a hint of trend in Ratchet Bob's abode. The yard, giant in comparison, was filled with lawnmowers, old boat motors, propellers, hunks of metal, and parts and pieces. Although crammed and decrepit-looking, the yard was carefully organized in a spiral pattern—lawnmowers around the edge, gradually circling to the boat and small engines in the middle.

"Um, hey," she said, desperately trying to remember anything from any cop show she'd ever seen, "I'm trying to determine my cousin Ricky—err, Richard's—whereabouts on Friday night. Are you able to corroborate his whereabouts?"

Ratchet Bob blinked at her.

"You on something, Biscotti?" he asked. "Drinking?"

Her face flamed with the heat of a thousand suns. This is not how this was supposed to go! Her interrogation technique was terrible.

"No. Um. Err…. were you with my cousin Ricky the other night?" Maybe the direct approach would have better results.

Bob crossed his arms, and Andrea got a whiff of sweat, grease, and more sweat. She tried not to wince.

"Yeah. We were doin work on Steve Jackman's boat." His eyes shifted and didn't meet hers. "He was helpin' me with the bilge pump."

"Steve Jackman's boat?" Andrea repeated.

"The Master Peace," Bob growled. "Big motorsailer. Red sails?"

That's the one. Her heart thudded heavily in her chest.

"How long were you there?" she asked. "And who's Steve Jackman?" As soon as the words came out of her mouth, she realized she did, in fact, know who Steve Jackman was.

Steve ran an art gallery in Nautic, Connecticut, right across the border. And now Steve Jackman was dead.

Bob scowled. "I was there til the ding-dang bilge pump was fixed," he grumbled. "It was late to start—bout seven-thirty, and we worked for over an hour."

"Did you see Steve?" Andrea asked.

"He was there when we started and was in the head when I left." Then his eyes narrowed. "What're you asking me all these questions for, girl?"

"I'm—" then a big blue truck pulled over. A guy stuck his head out the window.

"Hey, Bobby! My tractor needs attention. Can you come by?"

Ratchet Bob nodded. "This afternoon," he said.

He turned back to Andrea. "Look. Me and Ricky worked down below. Steve had some guys on the deck. We finished at around nine, and I left with Mike Rimbeau. Ricky was gonna change and go to some party. He was there when I left. That's what I told the police."

Bob and Andrea had the same realization at the same time: It was Ratchet Bob's words that caused Ricky to get picked up.

CHAPTER 10

Andrea left Ratchet Bob with a sick feeling in her stomach. Was her cousin the last person to see Steve Jackman alive? *That doesn't mean he killed him,* she admonished herself. But she could see why the police had talked with him, if he was the last person left on the boat with Steve.

Who *else* was on the boat with them? Who were the "some guys," besides Mike Rimbeau? She'd known Captain Mike, who she'd seen talking with Ricky in Didi's the morning of the chaos, for years.

Ricky was talking with Captain Mike!

She turned to glance at the Slip Shack. The Captain is Out sign hung on the door, and his flag was down. Not there. She'd have to go talk to him at some point. She should also probably go to Steve's art gallery later, even though it would likely be closed, but in the meantime there was work at Biscotti Realty to take care of—and she could watch the Slip Shack from there.

Lemon and Amaretto barely looked up when she came in. They snuggled together and resumed their naps.

Even though it was Sunday, Andrea had a bunch of messages to respond to, and as she listened to them she jotted notes of whom she needed to call back and built her to do list.

When she was done, she reviewed it. At first, she didn't even notice Item #3, but then:

Check bathroom faucet in Cottage 5—Ricky

jumped out. She covered her mouth with her hand. *Ricky!*

Her brain hadn't even realized that there was an issue. Ricky definitely wouldn't be helping with cottage five's faucet. Sadness and frustration crashed like waves inside her, swirling into an eddy of unsettling emotions.

Andrea made a couple of calls, but her backup handyman was busy, and so she left a message for her "do not call unless desperate" -guy. Finding someone reliable would not be easy the week before Boat Parade weekend.

Was there anyone else she could call? She gazed out the front window, not really paying attention to anything, just letting her mind wander.

The Mussels 4 Hire truck pulled up in front of the Sip n Scoop. Maybe Jack or one of the other guys might help with the faucet.

She was just about to call Jack, and then she remembered she had a dinner date with AJ that evening. Would that be awkward? And remembered AJ's impish grin.

The office door swung open, snapping her out of her daydream.

"Excuse me," the woman said. "Can you tell me if you do weekly rentals?"

"We do," Andrea said, adding in her head, *it's printed right on the door and the sign outside.*

The woman was tall—Madison tall. Over five foot ten, easily. She was wearing one of those designer dresses that the wealthy summer people love—the ones with the bright colored paisley and floral. Cut simply, Andrea knew they also ran about $175 in the downtown boutiques.

Andrea grabbed a rental agreement and gestured to her guest chair. Amaretto woke up and trotted over in the woman's direction.

"Is that your *pet?*" she asked from behind her giant white sunglasses.

Andrea smiled. "A tiny office mate," she said lightly. "He's well-behaved and will leave you alone."

Almost as if he'd heard her, Amaretto walked halfway across the room, lifted his nose in the air, gave a few sniffs, and turned and went back to bed, almost as if he'd smelled something that he didn't like.

Andrea could relate.

When she was done with Ms. Pretty Paisley dress—who decided not to book when she saw the size of the cottage—Andrea clipped the dogs' leashes on, flipped the sign to "closed" and headed out.

After taking their customary stroll through Front Street Park to check out the Slip Shack one more time—still closed—Andrea turned the boys around to put them back at the office instead of turning down Driftwood for the rest of their walk. Limoncello gave her a dirty look, as if to show her how he felt about cutting the walk short.

"Sorry, guys," she said, opening the door and letting them slip inside. "More tiny carrots for you later." The dogs loved the small carrots, and Andrea kept bags of them in the office fridge and at home. They were good for the pups—and occasionally she nibbled one, too.

She locked the door and went around back, where Daisy was parked. The bright blue Vespa scooter was her pride and joy. She put her helmet on, straddled Daisy's seat, revved up, and took off for Steve Jackman's gallery.

… and nearly crashed into a giant black SUV that was parked in the middle of Front Street. She swerved, then saw a sheepish Cordelia behind the wheel, trying to parallel park into a spot outside of her office.

"What the…?" Andrea muttered under her breath. Cordelia usually drove a small silver sedan, not this behemoth.

Maybe her car was in the shop? She made a mental note to ask her about the car switch if it was still there when she returned from her mission.

As she zipped along Front Street, Andrea turned questions over in her mind. What was Ricky doing, talking to Stephen Jackman? Why did he linger on the yacht? Who killed Jackman? Did he see it happen? Could her cousin actually have actually done something like this?

No way.

The Vespa puttered along, and Andrea pushed the worrisome thoughts from her mind. Getting information would help Ricky *and* settle her down. She took a couple of deep breaths of the ocean air and tried to focus on the ride.

It wasn't long before she crossed into Connecticut and wound onto the picturesque streets of Nautic. The historic town replicated its nineteenth-century heritage via its colonial building code. Much of the buildings were designed with weathered clapboard shingles and crisp white trim. A popular aquarium and colonial village ensured Nautic had tourists year-round, unlike Beach Hill.

Andrea turned onto Main Street and quickly spotted Well-Best Gallery. She parked Daisy, hung her helmet on the handlebars, shook out her hair, and gave the seat a quick pat before turning to the front of WellBest.

The oversized windows revealed a modern gallery space with white walls hung with modern paintings. A decal on one window listed the name of the artist and the show dates.

Andrea crossed to the door. Of course, there was a big "Closed Until Further Notice" sign on it. She didn't know what she expected—of course it would be closed!—but a knot of frustration formed between her shoulders.

She peered in to the gallery behind the sign, hoping to see someone. Focused on what was in front of her, when she felt the tap on her back, she shouted.

"Sorry," the tapper said, as Andrea spun. "I didn't mean

to startle you." The woman was petite—shorter than Andrea, even—and had a shock of pink bangs above dark sunglasses.

"It's okay," Andrea said. "I wasn't paying attention. Um, do you work here?"

In response, the woman took out a key ring and jingled it. "I do. But we're not open today."

"Oh, that's okay. I mean, I don't want to shop. Or look. Ummm…" Andrea stumbled over her words as she stepped aside to let the woman open the door. It swung in, and then the woman with the bangs scuttled over to a keypad to turn off the alarm.

Andrea, in a fit of bold decision-making, stepped into the gallery behind her.

"I'm hoping you can help me get some information about Steve Jackman," she blurted, as the gallery woman's eyes narrowed and lips pursed.

"Are you some reporter? Get out," she snapped.

"No! Not a reporter. I'm a realtor," said Andrea stupidly.

Pink Bangs cocked her head. "What does that have to do with anything?"

"Look, I'm just trying to find out what happened. Do you think you can give me a few minutes of your time and help me out?"

Pink Bangs studied Andrea. "Maybe," she said. "But I wasn't there, and I don't know what happened. Why are you poking around?"

What if, hearing that Ricky was being held, she decided not to talk to me?

Then I'm in the same boat I am right now.

Andrea squared her shoulders. "My cousin is being accused of the crime, and I don't think he could do something like that."

"So you're playing Nancy Drew?" Pink Bangs said coldly. "Nice."

Andrea shrugged, hoping the hopeless expression on her

face would convince this woman that she honestly meant no harm. "I'm just trying to help him out," she said.

Pink Bangs sighed, then glanced out the window, as though looking for an escape.

"Okay. I'll give you ten minutes."

Andrea tried to be chill. Her first real interview! She should've prepared better.

"Um, okay. So, I'm Andrea," she began. "And you are…?"

"Janess," the woman said. She crossed the gallery, her heels clicking on the floor, and went to a desk. She sat and pointed to a spindly-looking chrome and black chair on the opposite side. Andrea lowered herself carefully.

She opened her bag and fished for her notebook. *There is no way to make this look cool.* She sighed, grabbed her pen, and pulled it out. Janess raised one eyebrow at its sparkly exterior.

"Told you I'm not a pro," Andrea said in response.

"Sure aren't. What do you want to know?"

For a second, Andrea's mind went blank. She had no idea. Then, it came to her:

"Tell me what you told the police."

Janess sighed. "Fine."

Andrea settled herself and got ready.

Janess: Gallery Director
Statement

She printed at the top of the page.

"Let's go," she said.

"What I told the police was that Steven was kind of a jerk, and I'm not surprised someone killed him."

CHAPTER 11

A ndrea was so surprised that she nearly dropped her pen.
"What?"

Janess shrugged. "It's true. Guy was mean to everyone,
unless they were going to buy something. Then he was sweet
as pie and kind as a kindergarten teacher." She rolled her eyes.
"It was all just an act. This place is tanking. I'm not sure how
he was paying my salary, but as long as the check hit my
account, I showed up to work for the next week. I told Steve
that ages ago, when I realized that there was no way this place
made enough to cover the rent, let alone turn a profit."

"'Let me worry about that,' he said, and so I did." Janess
stared off into space, or at the multi-colored abstract painting
on the far wall, Andrea couldn't tell which.

"What about the other night?" Andrea prodded. She felt
just like a TV detective, asking the question.

Janess shrugged. "I mean, it was kind of normal. I was
here for the whole day—we open at eleven Thursday and
Friday, and close at eight. Steve came in around two, did some
paperwork, then left at around five. He said he was going to
take The Master Peace out to Beach Hill. He's never brought
me on the boat," she added bitterly.

"And now you'll never get to go out on it," Andrea added without thinking. *Oops!*

But Janess didn't seem to mind. She gave a dry laugh. "That's for sure," she said.

"Can I see his office?" Andrea asked. It seemed like a detective thing to do.

"I guess, but the police have it taped off so you can't go in." Janess led Andrea up a black metal staircase to a loft-like area above the gallery. A small restroom was at the top of the stairs, and just beyond it was Steve Jackman's office. Yellow police tape zigzagged across the door frame.

"Take a peek."

Andrea stood a few inches away from the tape and leaned forward as though peering through a fence. Jackman's office was white, like the rest of the gallery. A big black desk covered in papers and manila folders was on the left side of the room, a large monitor on top, a file cabinet next to it. A painting of a garden scene hung over the filing cabinet. To the right was a seating area with two small uncomfortable-looking orange chairs and a spindly coffee table. A large abstract painting with bars of bright colors hung above the chairs, facing the desk.

"Okay," Andrea said, jotting down the basics of the room in her notebook. She wished she could open drawers or poke around the gallery files. *I really am Nancy Drew!* she thought.

Janess escorted her downstairs and fussed with papers on her desk like she was ready for Andrea to leave. Andrea didn't care to take the hint and sat down again.

"Did Steve get or make any calls that day?" Andrea tapped her marker on the edge of the notebook, fighting the urge to chomp on the end, like she did with all of her pens when she was at her desk. That'd be a bad look.

Janess nodded. "Right before he left. He took it in his office, though, so I don't know who it was. He was agitated when he hung up. That's when he started talking about the boat and left."

Andrea frowned. "You have no idea who he was talking to?"

Janess shook her head. "Nope."

Andrea, frustrated, dropped her gaze to Janess's desk. It was neat, with a red folder in the center, a small jar of black pens—only black pens, the same black pens (*who only has one kind of pen on their desk?*)—and a boxy black phone with a bunch of buttons and a big display screen, just like the one she had at the office.

"Hey!" she said. "That's the same phone I have at work. There's a way to scroll back through recent calls… can I give it a try?"

Janess shrugged. "Sure. I don't care." She pushed back to make room.

Andrea popped up from her chair and came around the desk, squeezing close to Janess, but not even paying attention. Her fingers tingled. A clue!

She hit the "Recent calls" button, and the screen lit up with a number, whether it was incoming or outgoing, and the time and date. She pushed the back button to Friday, then carefully jotted down each number that popped up. There weren't that many.

"That's my mom," Janess said, pointing to one. "She never calls my cell while I'm at work because she says it's 'rude.'" A few more blinked by.

"There! That one!" The time stamp was 4:37pm. The area code was from Rhode Island. Andrea copied the numbers, plus the time stamp. She snapped a picture of the display with her phone for good measure.

"Do you recognize this number?" she asked Janess.

Janess shook her head. "Sorry, no clue. But I bet you can find it online."

Andrea nodded. "I bet you're right. And I know just who to ask to help me out."

CHAPTER 12

S he wrapped up with Janess and headed back to Daisy.
Before she took off for home, she checked her phone.
There were a bunch of missed video chats and texts from
Madison, and one text from AJ.

Still on? 7:30, Ocean Front?

She checked the time. *Yikes!* Barely enough time to get the
boys from the office, get home, feed them, and get ready to go.
She wished she'd made time to take a nap, too. The early start
to the day was killing her.

She hopped on Daisy and turned on the motor. As she was
about to pull away, she spotted Janess's shock of pink hair in
the gallery's door.

"One more thing!" Janess yelled. Andrea cut the ignition
and took off her helmet.

"One more thing," she repeated, coming to the parked
scooter. "Steve took a small charcoal gray duffel with him
when he left, and he hadn't brought it in with him that day. I
can't figure out what he took from the gallery."

Andrea thanked her and filed that away. Had the police
found the bag on the boat? How would she know? Was it even
important?

She puttered off and turned everything that Janess said

over in her mind on her ride. Finding out who called Steve Jackman was key.

Once she got back to the office, she grabbed the dogs—who were thrilled to see her—loaded them in the car, and finally returned Maddie's video call when she took the dogs out at home.

The superstar picked up on the second buzz, her face filling the screen, flawless skin basically glowing.

"Andrea!! Where are you? I've been trying to get you all day!"

"I know," Andrea replied. "Things have gotten… interesting… around here this weekend. When are you coming in to town?"

"Surprise! I'm here!" Maddie squealed. She pulled the phone back and swung it in a dizzyingly wide arc, through which Andrea identified the open and airy living room in Maddie's mansion. "I decided I wanted to do some unpacking myself. Come overrrr."

"Can't," Andrea huffed. Amaretto pulled them over to a very interesting telephone pole. "Going to dinner tonight. I can come by tomorrow?"

"How about after? Who are you going to dinner with?"

Oh. Ummmm… should she tell Maddie? She didn't want it to be weird or anything. AJ was her employee…? Or something?

Maddie's eyes darted from the screen. "Hey, I gotta go," she said. "There's a… situation going on over here. Come by tonight. I'll be up." The call ended, the black screen reflecting Andrea's surprised expression.

Limoncello barked his fool head off as a squirrel dared to cross the road in front of them. "Shhh!" Andrea said. "Leave the poor thing alone." Lemon gave her a withering glare, as if to say, *You kill all my fun, Woman.*

. . .

Once she squared the dogs away, she checked the time. Barely twenty minutes to get ready for her date! She'd worn her favorite dress to Uncle Eddie's party, and hadn't had a chance to drop it at the dry cleaner.

Andrea ripped into her closet like a tornado, flinging pants and tops onto her bed. A quick look, and she settled on black pants and a patterned boatneck top with sleeves that were floaty and fun.

She hopped in the shower, got dressed, fed the dogs, and did something to her tangle of curls that passed for hair. A swipe of mascara and lip gloss, and that was it.

If he liked what he saw enough to ask me out after I'd moved Madison in, this will be of an improvement, at least.

She let Amaretto and Limoncello out again, both dogs looking at her reproachfully for cutting their time outside short, and then dilemma: Take Daisy, and get windblown but find parking, or drive and likely park in the lot a block away from the Ocean Front, anyway?

Daisy won, helmet hair be darned.

She fired up her scooter and took off, buzzing towards Front Street.

The Ocean Front Bar & Grille was at the far, far end of Front Street—past Didi's dark windows, past the park and Melville's nest, past the antique shop, and the stretch of houses before the retail shops.

There was no parking out front—or anywhere that she could see—so Andrea was pleased with herself for choosing Daisy.

She parked the scooter on the sidewalk a few yards down from the restaurant, likely out of the way of pedestrians, and did her best to fix her hair in the reflection of a car window parked at the curb. Her curls were everywhere. She shook her head, regretting her decision to take the scooter.

As she opened the door to the restaurant, her stomach

fluttered with excitement. She briefly reflected that he'd been much more relaxed with Jack the night before last. Was that a good sign? Or were her nerves a bad one?

She didn't have time to give it any more thought, because as soon as she walked in, she spotted AJ, sitting at a table for two off to the side of the restaurant, with a beautiful view of the water.

"Hey there," he said.

"Hi," she said shyly. He pulled a chair out for her—*a gentleman!*—and Andrea settled herself. They chatted for a few minutes, then Andrea blurted, "If I have a telephone number, can you help me find out who it belongs to?"

AJ's mouth dropped open, then he laughed. "Okay, that's not weird or stalker-like behavior," he said. "Do I want to know more details?"

Andrea flushed. "Sorry," she said. "It's a little crazy…" She thought for a minute, and then decided—really, based on nothing but her intuition—that she could trust him.

She told AJ everything: About the party, Steve Jackman's murder, Ricky's alleged involvement, her conversation with Ratchet Bob, and then ending with Janess and the phone number. Their poor server had come by three times to take their order and had been waved off each time. Finally, as Andrea wrapped up the bit about Janess following her back outside, the server came back a fourth time.

"Look," she interrupted. "Are you eating?"

"So sorry," AJ said, "We are." They grabbed their menus and ordered quickly. The server huffed off.

The break gave Andrea a hot second to regret her choices. What had she been *thinking*, spilling her guts to this guy that she didn't know, maybe shouldn't trust, kind of liked, and now would most likely think she was a crazed lunatic stalker? AJ looked like he was about to say something, and she held her breath, waiting for him to laugh at her or just run away.

"That's amazing," he said. "What a story! And it's pretty easy to reverse look up a phone number…"

Andrea barely heard the rest, she was just so excited that he didn't run away from her! AJ had his phone on the table, and a couple of taps later, they had... nothing.

Just a number—and a big plate of fried calamari to nosh on while they talked.

"It's a burner phone," AJ. said. "There's no way to find out who owns it."

Andrea frowned. "What do you mean?"

AJ stabbed a calamari ring with his fork and chewed. "You can walk into any gas station and buy a cheap cell phone. You don't have to show ID or anything. Totally anonymous."

"That sounds shady."

"Bingo." AJ pointed at her with his fork. "So whoever's behind that burner phone likely knows something."

"But there's no way for us to figure out who that is," Andrea said glumly.

The server had removed the calamari and replaced it with her seared salmon. AJ had ordered a mixed seafood dish with lots of tentacles waving off the plate. Looking at it made Andrea a little queasy. Growing up in a seaside town, she loved seafood—but could only handle her calamari fried, not "friendly", as she called it.

AJ seemed to sense her discomfort and pushed some of the offending appendages deeper into his bowl.

"So now that we've stalked this guy and figured out there's a mystery caller, let's talk about what you think will actually happen."

"What do you mean?" Andrea said, then took a bite of salmon.

AJ stabbed into his bowl and came up with a shrimp on his fork. He waved it as he spoke. "Your cousin is a suspect. You've found out info that the police may or may not have about the call Steve got before he left the gallery, and you have a piece of evidence in the refrigerator in your office. This is totally not going to get you in trouble." AJ sounded serious, but his deep brown eyes were lit with a twinkling light as he spoke. Andrea was thoroughly swept away.

He popped the shrimp in his mouth and regarded her with a raised eyebrow.

"Do I have that right?"

She grinned. "When you put it that way…"

He leaned closer to her. "I'm just saying, I think you'd better get the police involved sooner rather than later. If this were a movie, you'd be out to dinner with a hunky detective instead of me, and he would be your partner in murder-solving. As it is now, unfortunately, all you have is me."

The way he said that last phrase, "all you have is me," sent a delicious shiver down Andrea's spine. She played along.

"You are so right. I can't even believe I'm talking to you right now. I should be with Officer Helpful, the lady who gave me the info about the slips when I brought over the cinnamon rolls. Or Niles Needermeyer, my elementary school nemesis turned cop." She folded up her napkin as if she were going to leave.

AJ laughed. It was a high-pitched giggle, one that she wouldn't have expected to come out of a grown man. It made her grin.

"Fair," he said. "But maybe you should reach out to him—or someone—soon, so things won't get too out of control."

Andrea swirled the wine in her glass. "I'll take that under advisement."

"Now, enough talking about that," AJ continued. "This was supposed to be a date, so let's talk about not-murder stuff…"

The rest of the night passed in a blur. Andrea laughed and chatted, learning about how AJ started working for Madison —the company he worked for sent him out to wire her Pacific Palisades house, and she offered to hire him on the spot—a little about his family (one brother, parents work for a financial company)—and how he liked Rhode Island (unexpectedly charming).

Sooner than she expected, Andrea was escorted to Daisy.

"This is yours?" AJ said, the surprise in his voice barely contained.

Andrea wound her hair in a bun and pulled on her helmet. "She sure is!" She hopped on the scooter. "No parking issues."

AJ admired the Vespa, then leaned against a street sign and smiled at Andrea.

"I had a great time tonight," he said. "Despite the stalking."

"Despite? Or because of?" Andrea shot back.

"I'll never tell," AJ said. He leaned closer. "Let's do this again?"

Andrea nodded. "Definitely, if you're in Rhode Island," she said.

"I'll be here for a bit." AJ tilted his head. "It's unexpectedly attractive." There was a long pause, during which she was hoping he'd kiss her... and then he gave a funny bow and stepped back. She turned Daisy's key and AJ backed up further.

"See you soon," she said.

"See you soon," he echoed.

She gave him a wave, then pulled out onto Front Street and headed towards home. Dinner with AJ left her with a heady, buzzy glow, and it surprised her to realize that she didn't want to go home alone and end the night, even though this had been the longest day in history.

Maybe I'll go to Madison's after all, she thought. But first she'd need to zip home and let the dogs out.

CHAPTER 13

An hour or so later, she let herself in the gate, using the opener Maddie had given her. She'd opted for her car instead of Daisy, because she'd also changed into blue and yellow rubber duck jammies and didn't love the idea of zipping around Beach Hill in novelty loungewear.

The dogs had given her a reproachful look when she left. She felt a little guilty, even though she'd left them each with a cookie.

I'm here! she texted Maddie

Come in were in the den came the response. Andrea was just as annoyed by the missing apostrophe as she was curious about the "we" in the sentence. She opened the big front door, and, unable to contain her excitement, called out, "I had such a great *daaayte*! Wait'll you hear with *whoooo*!" in a sing-song voice as she walked through the foyer, hall, and rounded the corner into the den.

"I hope it was with me," AJ said from his perch on an overstuffed chair.

A stone sank into the pit of Andrea's stomach, and her face got hot.

"Awkwardness abounds," Madison said from her spot on the floor.

Andrea wanted to melt into a puddle and evaporate. "Uhhh…"

Madison laughed. "Sit down; come on. It's fine."

Andrea forced herself to the couch, not making eye contact with AJ. *At least I'm still wearing a bra, she thought, even if I'm in my—*

"Nice jammies," AJ said.

Just kill me.

"I'm happy you two met and had a good time together," Madison said grandly from the floor pillow. "Now I think we should make popcorn and watch a horribly cheesy movie, because that is what normal people do with their friends and I have not had a normal person week."

Andrea nodded and glanced AJ's way. He was draped sideways in his chair, legs dangling over the arm, relaxed and slightly amused by the circumstances.

Andrea was not amused.

She perched on the edge of a chair on the opposite side of the room, as far away from AJ as she could get, and willed herself to disappear.

"At last now I don't have to worry about what kind of impression I made," AJ teased. Andrea tossed one of the chair's silk throw pillows at him. He caught it easily and grinned.

"I had a great date, too," he said. Andrea relaxed a little, sinking into the pillows at her back. Maybe this wasn't the most awful thing to have happened after all.

"Now. That movie." Madison rattled off the titles of five movies that Andrea swore were still in the theaters. "Screeners," she said, seeing Andrea's expression. "I'm a voting member of the academy because of Country Bumpkin. I'm supposed to watch these and vote for the Oscars." She shrugged while Andrea and AJ exchanged glances.

"Normal people don't get to watch screeners on movie night," Andrea pointed out. "If you want a normal-person night, we should watch what's streaming or whatever."

Madison cocked an eyebrow at her. "I don't want to be *that* normal." Andrea giggled.

"You ladies choose," AJ said, standing. "I'll go make popcorn." He stretched—Andrea glimpsed taut, warm brown skin as the hem of his shirt lifted—and then sauntered from the room.

"Which one?" Madison said, eyes twinkling, holding the DVDs in a fan.

Andrea selected one randomly. "That one. *I can't believe you invited him!*" She said the second part in a whisper-yell.

"You didn't *tell* me you were going out on a date with him," Madison pointed out. "How was I supposed to know not to?"

Fair point, but Andrea didn't like it.

"Look! You can snuggle with him under a blanket, since you picked the," she read off the DVD sleeve, "'scariest movie of the past hundred years' for us to watch."

Great. Andrea hated horror movies.

Before she could protest, AJ came back in with the popcorn. "Let's fire this up!" he said.

"Well, I'll never sleep again," AJ said cheerfully from his spot at the far end of the blanket.

"Is it over?" Madison's muffled voice came from behind the pillow she'd been hiding behind for the last twenty minutes.

"Finally," Andrea said, exhausted. Midway through the movie, when the heroine found herself trapped in the seaside mansion with her ex-husband's murderous spirit, they'd all moved to the floor pillows, grabbing a giant sherpa blanket to pull up to their chins. Madison was in the middle. "That's nightmare fuel for the next month."

"Let's talk about something else," Madison said, flinging the blanket off and sitting up in one motion. The rush of cold air made Andrea shiver.

She didn't really want to talk. She wanted to go to bed, even if she couldn't sleep. She snuck a look at the clock and cringed. It had been a long day, and "today" was stretching pretty deeply into tomorrow. Was this how all celebrities lived?

Andrea stifled a yawn. "What do you want to talk about?"

"I need something for that wall," Madison said, pointing across the room at the blank expanse over the overstuffed sofa. "Something coastal but not cheesy, you know?"

"There's a gallery on Front Street," AJ offered helpfully. He'd moved back to his chair. Andrea could see the dark shadows under his eyes from where she sat. She was pretty sure she looked just as tired.

She was also pretty sure Madison would hate everything at Gallery Sea. The owner, Ruthie Charles, was a lovely woman, but the sunset seascapes and driftwood art that she favored would not be Madison's taste.

"There's a place in the next town over," she said, immediately thinking of Janess and WellBest. There had to be something there that would appeal to her—and it might get her closer to the mysterious caller.

AJ caught her eye and grinned. "Yes! You should go there."

"I'm guessing this has to do with the detective situation you are in," Madison said to both of them. "I want full details."

"I'll fill you in tomorrow—er, later today," Andrea said, not even bothering to stifle her yawn this time. "The boys won't care that I've been up half the night." She stood and stretched, then turned to Madison.

"Want to go to that gallery tomorrow?"

Madison nodded, covering a yawn.

Celebrities—they're just like us! Andrea thought, stifling a giggle. Before she could say anything stupid out loud, she gave AJ a dorky half-wave and grabbed her stuff.

He was next to her in an instant. "Let me walk you out," he said.

Andrea furrowed her brow. "But… we're at Madison's house. I doubt there are any murderers out there. Or even evil paparazzi. The worst that's outside is a grouchy raccoon."

AJ wore a very serious expression. "Grouchy raccoons are *extremely dangerous*. I'd better make sure you're okay." He gently looped his arm through hers, and that's when Andrea realized he was interested in spending more time with *her*. In spite of her exhaustion, her heart quickened.

When they were outside, just beyond the glow of Madison's porch lights, AJ pulled his arm from hers. Andrea had found it so warm and natural there that she stopped in front of her car. She turned to him.

"I should have done this earlier. Thank you for a lovely night. Please excuse my popcorn breath," AJ said. Then he leaned in and brushed her lips with his.

"You're excused," Andrea squeaked, once the warm tingling sensation faded a little and she got her wits about her again. "But maybe we should do that again without popcorn breath?" She hoped he didn't take her jokey barb as serious and get offended.

"Absolutely."

Relief, mingled with excitement, shot through Andrea.

"We'll figure out the details tomorrow…. today… later," he said.

Andrea smiled. "Sounds like a plan." He stepped back and she got in her car, taking a minute to gather herself before turning on the ignition. He was right there when she looked up. She gave him a big smile, then pulled down Madison's long driveway, too excited to sleep.

CHAPTER 14

Andrea was wrong: She did, in fact, go to sleep when she got home. The next morning—or later that day—she still had that happy, warm feeling after AJ's kiss.

But she also had another problem: Jack. What was she going to do about him? He was definitely cute, but he didn't make her heart go pitter-patter the same way that AJ's did. And he lived in Beach Hill. Who knew how long AJ would stay?… And there was still a matter of her cousin Ricky being blamed for Steve Jackman's murder. Not to mention the evidence in her fridge.

As AJ pointed out, there was a lot to consider.

Andrea took the dogs out for those for their customary walk on the beach. That's when she did her best thinking. *Another list.* She needed a list. She and the dogs walked down Front Street. It was a beautiful sunny morning, although a bit later than she was used to.

Okay, back to that list. AJ was going to call her today. She knew *that* was one thing on her list.

Then there was Jack.

She had to talk to him herself, so she should probably call him.

And there was the gallery visit with Madison.

After that came the murder stuff. She needed to talk to Captain Mike. He had been on the boat. Maybe he'd seen or heard something before he left with Ratchet Bob? Then there was the hat. Should she turn it in? Maybe the officer with the cinnamon roll *was* actually her best chance for getting that into the police department, because she didn't want to deal with Niles Needermeyer. She'd have to think about it a little more.

After her walk, she brought the dogs over to Didi's Tea Shoppe and tied them up outside. Lemon gave her a dirty look. He loved the smell of the shop and wanted to go in, but he was not welcome—at least, not during the high season. Didi let her sneak her dogs in when things were quieter in the winter time, but it was not cool to bring them in during the summer.

"Just wait right here. I won't be gone long," she said, giving Amaretto a pat on the head. "I just have to run in and get my hot chocolate and talk to Didi."

The bell over the door jingled as she went inside. Every seat was full. DiDi's steaming cinnamon buns stood in the case, some type of berry scones next to them. Andrea set her eyes on those.

"Hello stranger," Didi said. "Do you have the boys with you?" Andrea nodded. Didi pulled out a to go cup. "Well, you're gonna need one of these, hun." Andrea watched as gratefully as Didi filled the cup with steaming hot chocolate. Di snapped the lid on it, then slid it across the counter to Andrea.

"What happened with the date?"

Andrea explained everything to Di quickly and softly as she could so that the other customers wouldn't hear. Di listened, filling the occasional order with eyes wide.

"What are you going to do?" Di asked.

"About Ricky? I don't know."

"No, I mean about AJ and Jack?"

"I can see where your priorities are."

"Well, I can see where yours should be," she said. Andrea giggled. "And now that that's out of the way, did you hear about that Coast Guard situation?"

Andrea took a sip. "Uh, no. Fill me in, please."

A buzzer went off. Di held up a finger, then disappeared into the kitchen, presumably to take something delicious from the oven. She returned with a fresh berry scone on a plate.

"Give it a sec," she said, as Andrea went for the pastry. "The Coast Guard situation. Boo heard it on that scanner app he loves. Evidently, the Lazy Sunday was found adrift last night. They sent a rescue boat for it."

Andrea, who had stuffed a steaming piece of scone in her mouth, raised her eyebrows. She swallowed. "Came unmoored?" Rarely, but sometimes a boat wasn't tied properly and it floated off its mooring. The Coast Guard would tow it in.

Boo chose that moment to pass by them with a refill for the coffeepot. He turned to Andrea and gave her a shrug.

Di cocked her head. "That's where it gets interesting. Boo said the scanner feed went dark."

"Hmmm." Andrea didn't know what to do with that info, but figured she'd ask Capt. Mike if he knew what happened to the Lazy Sunday when she got around to talking to him.

Andrea thanked Di for the croissant and info, paid for her hot chocolate, bought the boys peanut butter bones and started her walk home with the dogs. The Steve Jackman thing was growing more and more complicated. And now there was the Lazy Sunday. Was that somehow related?

Ugh. It's too much.

Then there was the situation with AJ and Jack. Much as she didn't want to admit it, Di was right. She had to figure out who she was going to pursue. She didn't want to hurt anyone's feelings. But in her heart, Andrea knew AJ was the one who made her get all a-flutter.

By the time she got home, she had somewhat of a plan: Text Jack. Have him come to the office after school to break it

to him gently, and hope that Madison had so many IT problems that AJ would be a frequent visitor.

When Andrea got to the office, she had sent Jack a text and he
responded he would be over later in the afternoon. Just *thinking*
about talking with him made Andrea feel queasy, but at the
same time she was looking forward to the relief of having the
conversation out of the way.

To distract herself, tackled the remaining tasks getting the
rentals organized for the boat parade, contacting potential
renters for later in the summer, and figuring out who was
going to do the final repairs on the cottages while Ricky was
unavailable.

As the day went on, she got more and more nervous. She
even skipped lunch. By the time the school day ended, she was
jittery and stressed. *This won't do.* To steady herself, she went
into the back of the office, into the bathroom, and grabbed
the sink with both hands. She took a deep breath and looked
in the mirror.

"You can do this," she said to her exhausted reflection.
"It's OK that he's totally cute, totally nice, and local. It's OK
that you have no chemistry with him. It's OK, even though if
it doesn't work out with AJ you'll never be able to date Jack
again. And it's OK that if it doesn't work out with AJ you'll
just be alone for the rest of your life with your dogs." She
rolled her head and neck a little like a boxer preparing for a
fight. The bell at the door tinkled. Her stomach immediately
clenched and she felt less like a boxer and more like a wimp.
Come on, girl! She tried to breathe, then stepped out of the
bathroom into the main office.

Madison was sitting in her office.

"It's you?" Andrea said, her voice coming out more
screech than regular hello.

"I thought you'd be happier to see me," said Madison
dryly. She was wearing a lavender Beach Hill hoodie, a pair of

white jeans, and cute little pink shoes. A little closer to fitting in, but Andrea knew that sweatshirt had been tailored to fit her just so and there was no way anyone local in Beach Hill would wear cute kitten heeled pink shoes in May.

A rush of relief had followed had followed the initial arrival of Madison, Andrea had to admit. But, as soon as the relief came, it was replaced by a whole other level of anxiety: Jack was going to show up any minute! And she was going to break up with him. She couldn't do that if Madison was in her office—Madison, who was supposed to come by at lunch, which was hours ago.

Her friend had clearly been waiting for Andrea to say something. And when she didn't, she dove in on her own.

"We talked about going over to that gallery together at lunch," she said. "I slept in. Didn't you say it was in the next town over?" Her eyes were hopeful.

Oh, no. Madison thought she was upset with her for being late. *Why can't I get anything right today?*

"Oh, honey, it's not you. It's just that…"

Right then was when the door opened. This time, it really *was* Jack. He walked in wearing khaki pants and a blue and white checkered button-down shirt, all twinkling blue eyes and big smile. Andrea's heart melted and, much to her surprise, she saw Madison's eyes widen.

"Oh hey," Jack said. "I hope I'm not interrupting anything?"

"No, of course not." Andrea said. "I want you to meet my friend Madison."

Madison stood, all five-foot-ten of her rising like a golden goddess. She held her hand out to Jack. "Nice to meet you."

That's when Andrea realized they were the only two people in the room. There was an electricity between them that crackled. If she didn't know better, she would've thought that her computer fried. At first she felt a twinge of jealousy—after all, Jack was here so she could break up with *him*. But then she realized, maybe this would solve all her problems! If

Jack fell for Madison, then he wouldn't care so much about Andrea not wanting to see him anymore. But would Madison, who had once dated two male models at the same time (according to the tabloids), really go for some guy who taught elementary school and worked part time as a construction worker?

Andrea came back to herself. The whole time she had been thinking, they had been talking. Madison was looking up at Jack with her enormous blue eyes, and he had a dopey grin on his face as he looked down at her.

"So Madison, did you wanna check out that gallery?" Andrea asked, just to insinuate herself into the conversation.

"Oh, well…" Andrea couldn't believe it. Madison seemed… *Flustered?!*

"Andrea, I don't want to interfere if you already have plans," Jack said.

"Well, I don't know about you, but I'm hungry." said Madison, apparently losing all interest in art.

Andrea looked at them and realize that this was a perfect opportunity.

"Oh no," she said. "I am *so* sorry, but just before you got here, Madison, I had a big issue with one of the renters for the boat parade. I have to make some phone calls and get a few things sorted out. Why don't you two go and I will catch up with you when I'm done?"

Jack and Madison exchanged glances like they simultaneously weren't sure if they should go and couldn't wait to get out of the office.

"How does the tea shop sound?" Jack asked, evidently deciding not to pass up the opportunity.

"Sounds great," Madison replied.

The way she was looking at him, Andrea thought Madison would've gone to the junkyard with Jack had he asked. Jack and Madison murmured goodbyes in her direction. Jack held the door for Madison, and they stepped out onto the sidewalk.

When the door closed behind them Andrea let out a bark of a laugh.

That was easier than I thought.

Had Jack really fallen for Madison? *OK*, she told herself, *let's be real.* Of *course* Jack would fall for Madison! Madison was a star—literally. And she was beautiful, smart, and funny.

Andrea laughed out loud. Who'd have thought that having the cute guy that you went on a date with getting stolen away by a musician could feel so good? The situation was straight out of a Hollywood story. Maybe the Madison–Jack thing wouldn't last, but at least for now, it made Andrea's life easier. And easier was definitely what she needed. A weight lifted off her shoulders and she hoped, really, truly hoped, things would work out. Madison deserved someone normal and kind, and Jack, well, any guy would be happy to go on a lunch date with Madison the superstar.

All that was left was this whole murder situation and her cousin Ricky. And really, Ricky honestly couldn't kill somebody. She's known him literally her whole life. He was also kind and came from a good family. What did he have to kill anybody for?

Andrea almost had herself convinced to just let everything go and set up another date with AJ. It would be easy to just laugh everything off and move on with her day, except for the fact that her cousin had been held by the police the other day. And she had his baseball cap in her office refrigerator.

So what to do, then?

There was only one option left: she had to talk to Ricky herself. For whatever reason, that prospect filled her with dread. It's not that she thought that he'd be mad at her, but even though they were cousins, she had a business relationship with him. She was his boss, kind of. She hired him to do the maintenance on the cottages every year. He was Mr. Fix-it when anything went wrong, and he'd always been reliable and showed up and done whatever she needed. And then when they were at a family event they could be cousins again—laughing, teasing, and joking. It had been easy to separate the two. If she came at Ricky and interviewed him as being a murder suspect, the relationship with him as a cousin certainly wouldn't change—would it? But her relationship with him as his employer definitely could.

CHAPTER 15

A ndrea brought the dogs home, threw on a light jacket and decided that she would take Daisy over to Ricky's place. The sun on her shoulders warmed her through the jacket and she enjoyed the view zipping up and away from the beach, climbing the gentle hill that let away from the water, out of the downtown area. Ricky lived in an apartment ground floor of a house that was owned by Andrea's aunt and uncle. Gwen lived upstairs. When she pulled up, the whole house was shut off tight — on this bright sunny day curtains were drawn, and it looked dark and sad. Andrea took her helmet off, hung it on Daisy and then climbed the front steps. She hit the buzzer for Ricky's apartment and waited. And waited. No response.

Andrea stepped back away from the door, and leaned to either side to see if she could see in the windows. Curtains, or whatever was on the other side, closed the view. So she hit Gwennie's buzzer instead. A few moments later she heard someone yell, "hold on a minute." Footsteps came down the stairs. Gwennie appeared in the window, peeking out before she opened the door.

"Hey Andrea," she said.

Andrea smiled, and asked "Is Ricky here?"

She nodded. "He's upstairs. We were hanging out." She pointed up the staircase behind her. Andrea followed Gwennie up the stairs and into her apartment. The apartment was a lot like Gwennie herself – bright, colorful, and tastefully put together in ways that Andrea could never manage. But even still, something was off about it. All of Gwennie's funky printed curtains were drawn against the beautiful late spring day. Andrea decided not to say anything.

Her cousin, who she was there to see, was slouched the end of Gwennie's table clutching a cup of coffee like it was a life preserver. He barely glanced up when she came in. Gwen busied herself making tea.

"How's it going?" she immediately felt stupid for saying anything because it sounded totally wrong. How *could* it be going when you were suspected of murder?

Ricky turned to face her. He raised one eyebrow, and the dark circles under his eyes and the patchy stubble revealed his exhaustion.

"How do *you* think it's going?"

Andrea leaned forward. "Look, Ricky, I'm so sorry. I've asked around a little to see what I can find out. Steve Jackman seemed like a shady guy."

Before she could go on, Ricky ran his hands through his hair and made a frustrated noise. "What is *wrong* with you? These people, you don't even know — just stop. Stay out of it before you get me in more trouble."

Andrea hadn't expected this reaction from him. She knew that she wasn't a detective, but she would've thought that with their working relationship and how close they were, he would've at least felt grateful that she was trying to help. She pulled away and leaned back in her chair.

"Look, I'm just trying to figure out what happened. Someone called him before he went to the boat. If I can find out who made that call, maybe it can help you. if there's anything that I can do—any information I can give to somebody that will get you out of this—please tell me Ricky, and I'll do it."

Ricky put both hands on the table, eyes wide, leaning towards her and said in a low voice so that Gwennie couldn't hear, "Stay out of this Andrea. You don't know what you're getting into and I don't want you to get hurt." His eyes blazed, rage simmering under the surface.

Andrea couldn't believe what she was hearing, let alone when she was seeing. Ricky looked nothing like the cousin she grown up with or the person with whom she worked for nearly five years.

Flustered, Andrea stood and grabbed her bag. Her stomach churned. She just wanted to get out of that weird dark room and away from Gwennie and Ricky. She reached out as if to put her hand on her on his shoulder, and pulled it back. If she was being honest, a finger of fear stroked the back of her neck. She called out to Gwen that she was leaving turned her back on Ricky and let herself out downstairs.

Her phone buzzed as she was getting on Daisy. A text from Madison.

Lunch w Jack was [heart emoji - heart emoji] must talk!

Andrea grinned, then tucked the phone into her pocket and buckled her helmet. Was Madison Beech falling for a Rhode Islander? The paparazzi would have a field day with that.

The momentary laugh that gave her almost made up for the lousy interaction she'd had with Ricky. If she were being honest, he seemed kind of...*off*. She shook her head, not allowing herself to even think further than that, and started the moped.

And then it occurred to her: Ricky used the word "people" when referring to Steve Jackman. She was right—there were two people involved in whatever he had going on.

Couldn't be, she thought, as the engine puttered to life. She pulled onto the street and headed towards downtown Beach Hill, not exactly sure of where she was going next. She didn't want to race to follow up with Madison and Jack, she wanted answers about her cousin's involvement with Steve Jackman. As she drove, she turned over what she knew:

- Steve's business was in Connecticut, but he had a boat slip in Beach Hill.
- Steve got a call and left the gallery Friday night to head to the boat.
- The boat was lit up during Uncle Eddie's party.
- Jackman had a dark gray bag with him.
- Ricky was on the boat to help fix the bilge pump with Ratchet Bob.
- Capt. Mike Rimbeau was also on the boat.
- Ratchet Bob and Capt. Mike left, and Ricky was still on the boat with Steve.
- Andrea had Ricky's SeaDogs hat in her refrigerator.
- Janess had said Steve was a jerk to work for.
- Jackman's body had been found in the cove the next morning.

It was time to talk to Mike Rimbeau.

She piloted Daisy down Front Street towards the boathouse parking lot.

In larger communities, a harbormaster oversees the boats and rules of the slips and docks. Beach Hill was so small, they didn't use the term. The captain of the Slip Shack was Mike Rimbeau, a former competitive yachtsman who hurt his leg in a boating accident, and was rumored to have lost his winnings via some ill-placed bets on his former competitors. He ran the slips and ensured that boaters followed the rules in Beach Hill's cove.

Hopefully he's in today.

Andrea pulled up to the Slip Shack, a small, weathered gray building with white trim on the edge of the shore, near the yacht club. The "Captain is In" sign hung on the door.

Andrea pulled up on Daisy, cut the engine, and took off her helmet. She knocked.

"Yeah?" The gruff voice carried through the wooden door.

Andrea poked her head in. "Captain Mike?"

The captain sat behind a desk awash in papers. His face was deeply lined from years of being on the water, but his brown eyes twinkled when he saw her.

"Andrea! Come in! What brings you here?" He stood and crossed the small space, giving her a peck on the cheek.

Andrea had known Captain Mike for literally her whole life. He'd given sailing lessons to kids of Beach Hill for decades. She moved some papers off a chair and sat across from him.

"I'm hoping you can give me some information," she said. "About my cousin Ricky."

Mike shrugged and extended his palms to her. "I will if I can," he said.

"He's in trouble. The police think he's the one who killed Steve Jackman. I don't believe he could do something like that. There has to be a mistake. You were there that night; did you see anything?"

Captain Mike steepled his hands on his desk. "It's truly unfortunate. Your cousin's a good kid, but I'm afraid I can't be of much help. I told the police that I left with Ratchet Bob. Rick was still on the boat when I left."

Andrea shifted in her seat. "Well, first I was wondering why Steve has a slip here, in Beach Hill. Doesn't he live in Connecticut?"

Mike nodded. "He does. But his boat is registered here. Told me he didn't like the harbormaster in Niantic Harbor. Registered his boat here about three years ago."

Andrea nodded, and fished out her unicorn notebook to jot that down.

"Does anyone else from Niantic have a slip here?" She almost surprised herself with the question. Captain Mike rubbed his chin as he thought.

"Not that I can recall," he said. "We have two out-of-staters—both snowbirds who come up here for the summer and winter in Florida—but everyone else is based here in Beach Hill or other neighboring towns."

"But all in Rhode Island?" Andrea said.

Mike nodded. "All in Rhode Island," he repeated.

"Don't you think if the Niantic harbormaster were a jerk, you'd have more Connecticut people asking for slips?"

Mike cocked his head at her. "I hadn't thought about it at all until right now," he said. "And Wally Shores over in Niantic is not such a bad guy. Maybe Jackman got him on the wrong day?"

"Maybe," Andrea said out loud, but inside she was thinking about Janess's description of her boss. With all of those people hating him, maybe it was *him* who was the problem, not Wally Shores.

"Why were you on the boat that night? Was anyone else there?"

Mike took a short length of sail cord from the top of his desk. He looped and knotted it, untied it, then did it again. He glanced at Andrea. "Steve called and asked me to come pick up his slip lease for this summer. It renews Boat Parade weekend, like a lot of folks' around here. We talked about the bilge pump problem, I took the lease and that was it." Tie. Untie. "Bob and Rick wrapped up, and I left with Bob."

That matched pretty much everything she knew, but she thought she was missing something. Meanwhile, she caught a flicker of…something…come across Capt. Mike's face.

"What?" she prodded. "Is there something else?"

His eyes shifted to the desk, to the rope, back to her. "No. Why?"

There was more to this story, she knew it. "You have…a look," she said finally. "It's okay. I just want to know what happened."

Capt. Mike gave a big sigh, then smoothed the unkotted piece of cord on the desk. "It's not great," he admitted. "See, Ratchet Bob and I left, and your cousin was supposed to settle up with Jackman and go to some party." His eyes darted around the room.

Andrea leaned closer, heart thudding.

"I…heard raised voices," Mike said softly. "I stopped to check the cleat ties at another boat on the dock, and I heard a commotion coming from The Master Peace. I should've gone back to check, but I was tired and I mind my own business, you know?" His face was miserable. "I'm sorry, Andrea."

Numbness settled over her like a blanket. *You asked*, she admonished herself. *But an argument doesn't necessarily lead to murder*, she retorted. Andrea swallowed hard.

"Thanks," she said. She sat quietly for a moment, taking in the implications of his words. As she did, her eyes roamed the small space, settling on a flat, brown-paper wrapped package leaning against a filing cabinet. The return address was just visible, and Andrea recognized it as the street address of The WellBest Gallery. *What?!*

"What about that?" Andrea pointed. Desperation threatened the edge of her heart.

"What?" Mike followed Andrea's line of sight, landing on the package. He cleared his throat, then sat there.

"That." He was clearly holding something else back. "Maybe it's something that can help Ricky…"

Mike wiped his face with a large, scarred hand. "It's likely nothing to do with your cousin," he said. "but I didn't mention it to the police."

"I'll keep it quiet," Andrea said quickly. *Please, please let this help Ricky.* Because everything else was not looking so good.

"Jackman got a lot of packages here," Mike said, his voice lowered. "I…accepted them for him sometimes."

"What…kind…of packages?" Andrea asked, her heart and mind both racing. What did this mean? Was Jackman doing something illegal? Had Ricky found out?

Captain Mike flushed, his face going a brick red. "Just big flat ones. He said it was pieces of art for his gallery. I would never take anything illegal or…something," he finished lamely.

"Of course not," Andrea replied automatically. This was some good information. Why had Jackman been receiving art at the Beach Hill cove? Wouldn't that have gone to Janess? And why hadn't Captain Mike told the police? It must have been…

"You were taking money from him for accepting the deliveries, weren't you?" Andrea said out loud.

Captain Mike kept his eyes on the top of his desk. He gave a slow nod. "I was," he said.

"How often did they come?"

"About every other week," he said to the desk.

"And how much did he pay you?" Andrea let the question hang in the silence.

"Two hundred per delivery," he said. "But I didn't think anything of it," he said. "If it were drugs or something I would never have done it. But it was big flat paintings."

Andrea smiled at him. "Of course. No big deal." In the back of her mind, she kept hearing Janess talk about how broke Jackman was. *Did this have something to do with the money coming in to the gallery? Was Ricky involved? Is that what they were arguing about?*

"Did he pick them up?"

"Sometimes," Mike said. "But mostly it was his partner."

Partner? Steve Jackman had a partner?!

CHAPTER 16

"Wait a minute," Andrea said. "What do you mean, 'his partner' paid you or picked up the packages?"

Mike's eyes went wide, like he knew he'd given away too much. "It was just some guy," he said miserably. "Look, Andrea, if you tell the police about this I could lose my job. And what else am I going to do? I can't sail anymore. I just said I'd do it for a little extra cash."

Andrea couldn't care less why Mike did it or what he needed the money for. She wasn't even interested in telling the police about his involvement.

But she really, really wanted to know who the partner was.

"Can you tell me about the partner? What's his name?"

Mike shrugged. "He said his name was Riggs. Never gave me a first name. Just showed up the day after a piece was delivered, paid me in cash, and we loaded it up into his truck."

"What kind of truck?" Andrea said. She'd scooted forward to the absolute edge of her seat.

"A big blue pickup." Mike scribbled the make and model on a sheet of paper and passed it to her. He looked older than when she'd arrived, and his eyes had lost their twinkle.

"Thanks." She slipped the paper into her pocket and stood. "I appreciate it, Mike."

He shook his head. "I'm an idiot," he said. "I should've known better. And look, I don't know what your cousin and Jackman were arguing about, but I hope he gets clear of this."

Andrea patted him on the arm, not knowing what to say. She was pretty sure that they both knew that what he'd done was illegal, and although Andrea made a promise to herself that she wouldn't be the one to set the police on Mike, consequences might likely find their way to him. *Like they might find their way to Ricky?* a little voice in her head chirped. She ignored it.

She stepped to the door, then turned back.

"Was that the most recent delivery?" she asked, lifting her chin in the direction of the package.

Mike nodded, then blew out a big rush of air. "Yeah. It came the day Jackman was murdered," he said.

"And…?"

"And let's check it out," he finished.

Captain Mike led her around the back of the Slip Shack to a storage shed.

"It's where I keep the PFDs, cove markers, flashlights," he said. He twisted a key into the thick padlock that hung from the hasp. Andrea glanced around the dock. The police presence had died down, but some of the slips were still taped off. She hoped the tape would be down for the Boat Parade, and then felt a little guilty thinking that. Steve Jackman's killer needed to be brought to justice, no matter if it interfered with the start of Beach Hill's summer season.

Not a lot of people were out this afternoon, even though it was a bright, sunny May day. A gull screeched overhead, and the sharp tang of the ocean was on the air.

Mike juggled the lock and it popped open. The shed was shorter than the shack itself—about six feet tall or so, and Mike had to duck through the doorway. Andrea peered into the darkness. Shelves of rope, buoys, sail cloth, and assorted nuts, bolts, each neatly labeled with the equipment they held, lined the back wall. Mike grabbed a box cutter off a shelf, then went back into the slip shack. He carried the brown-wrapped package out of the shack and leaned it against the shed door. It was flat, and about four feet high by three feet wide.

"This is it," Mike said.

Andrea studied it: plain brown wrapping, about two inches thick, no markings. It certainly *looked* like a piece of art.

"Should we open it?" Mike asked.

"It's probably evidence, and it's probably a bad idea," Andrea said. "But…"

Captain Mike leaned the package against the outer wall of the shed, then went back in. He emerged with a pair of work gloves.

"We'll be careful," he said. He turned the object around, to where the folded flaps of the paper were taped down.

Slowly, he slid the knife under the flap, releasing the tape. He did the same for the other one, and Andrea's heart skipped beats. Then, he lifted the flap, unwrapping the back of the package.

Facing them was the plain brown backing of a picture frame, a wire stretched taught across its span.

"Huh," Andrea said. Mike shifted the frame so they could see the front. It was a painting of a garden done in an impressionist style. Not something that WellBest typically sold.

"All set?"

Andrea nodded. Mike carefully resealed the package, smoothing the tape down, and returned it to the storage shed.

"Will you call me if you hear from Riggs?" Andrea asked.

Captain Mike nodded.

"You know, you really should talk to the police about this," she said.

"I'm thinking it might be better for me to go to them before they find me," Mike said thoughtfully.

Andrea patted him on the arm. "I think so, too," she said.

But in the meantime, she had information that the police didn't have. And could this mysterious "Riggs" person be the one on Jackman's phone records? That would put him on the Beach Hill dock. With cash.

"Oh, one more thing," she said, turning back to him. "Do you know what happened with The Lazy Sunday?" She figured she could tell Di and the Boo.

Surprise flashed across his face, and another expression that she didn't recognize. "Oh, terrible situation, there. Found adrift, and the owner, a guy from Connecticut, was found dead onboard. Likely a heart attack. How do you even know about that?"

Andrea was taken aback. Another boat death! It was an accident, but still. "That's terrible," she said.

She climbed back on Daisy and headed home to let the dogs out, turning these new details over in her mind. Andrea knew there was a piece she was missing, but she couldn't see what it was yet. Everything hinged on Riggs, and what Ricky and Jackman were arguing about.

She hoped those answers would prove her cousin's innocence, and not make things even worse.

CHAPTER 17

Lemon and Amaretto were sitting right at the door, tails thumping, when she came in. Although they pressed against her legs and wagged enthusiastically, Andrea knew the dogs were annoyed with her.

Why'd you leave us here so long? Limoncello's expression said. *We stick together.*

"Sorry, buddy." Andrea scratched his ears and gave them each a tiny carrot. The dogs forgave her quickly.

She clipped their leashes on and decided to walk them to her office, so they'd be with her for the rest of the afternoon, although there wasn't much of it left. Stomach rumbling, she grabbed a cheese stick and handful of baby carrots for herself, hoping to swing by Didi's for dinner. Or a snack. Or whatever it would be by then.

But what about that painting, and Captain Mike's regular package reception for the mysterious Riggs?

Could those deliveries be how Steve Jackman was keeping the lights on at the gallery?

Where was the money going from and going to? Where did having Mike hold a painting and get paid two hundred dollars fit in?

Andrea mused as she walked, but the pieces still didn't fit. Who would want Jackman dead?

The boys stopped to sniff a hydrangea bush, and Andrea nudged them along. Amaretto gave his short, happy "I see you!" bark, startling Andrea out of her daydream.

The dog strained at the leash, nose twitching, Limoncello following his lead.

"Hey!" A white SUV with dark tinted windows rolled up to the curb, Madison at the wheel. Amaretto barked again.

Andrea crossed the street so she could lean into the passenger window.

"How was your late lunch?" she asked, grinning.

"You'd already know if you called me *back*." Madison pouted. Andrea had to remind herself that Madison was not used to waiting—and sometimes that meant Madison was not good at being patient.

"I was checking out some leads. Besides, I guessed from the tone in your voice that it went pretty well."

Madison turned pink. "Sure did. He's the sweetest. I'm going to have him over for dinner once the kitchen staff gets here and settled."

Andrea blinked. *Dating a superstar is very different from a night at the Waverunner.*

"So," Madison said, "about that gallery?"

Andrea glanced at the boys, who had trundled over to investigate the smells on a nearby fire hydrant. "I need to check in at the office and drop these guys off. Pick me up in about an hour?" She'd text Janess and hopefully get her to open the gallery if she weren't already there.

Maddison agreed and headed toward her estate. Andrea hurried the boys along, earning her an indignant look from Amaretto, who hated to be rushed.

"I'll make it up to you both with a long walk on the beach when this is over," she told them as she unlocked the door to Biscotti Realty. The boys ignored her, immediately stretched and took to their beds, curling up for a nap.

The voicemail light on her phone blinked angrily, and she took a breath before logging in to the messages.

Three were from prospective renters, two were from handymen who she'd asked to cover some of Ricky's work, and the last one—left only minutes before she'd arrived, was from the police station.

"Andrea Biscotti, this is Officer Needermeyer at the Beach Hill police department. We would like you to come down to the station. We have some questions for you."

Andrea rolled her eyes. "Officer Needermeyer".

Madison was coming to get her in an hour, and Andrea figured going back to the gallery would be a much better use of her time than sitting in the police office with Niles the Nose-Picker.

She'd call when they got back.

While she waited for Madison, she quickly returned the calls for the prospective renters, and made a to-do list for when she next sat down at her desk. Whenever that would be.

She also rang Janess. "I'm bringing an interested buyer over to the gallery. Are you open this evening?"

"I can be," she said.

Aside from taking Madison to get new art, Andrea also hoped that there was a clue there, something she was missing.

Amaretto stuck his head on her knee, soulful brown eyes on hers. She rubbed behind his ears, earning a blissed-out doggy expression and appreciative tail wag.

"Thanks, buddy," she said aloud. Amaretto always knew when she needed a little extra canine companionship to put her own issues into perspective.

Perspective. That was it!

A tingling thrill shot through her as she turned the idea over in her mind. How had she missed it?

She cupped Amaretto's head in her palms. "You're a genius!" she told him. "Best dog ever. No offense, Lemon!" she hastily added.

Andrea sprung up from her chair and gathered her bag,

checking for her pen and notebook. She was quickly getting attached to that sparkly unicorn.

Ready when you are, she texted Madison.

Instead of a response, a honk came from outside the office. She tossed a "see you boys later!" over her shoulder and slipped out the door.

She knew exactly what she was looking for at the gallery.

CHAPTER 18

The sun, low in the sky, sparkled on the water as they maneuvered down Front Street. Madison's SUV was not quite as big as the monstrosity that Cordelia was driving these days, but it was larger than most of the year-rounders' cars.

Where did this even come from? Andrea thought idly, stroking the buttery caramel interior. It had that new-car smell, and then Andrea realized: It *was* a new car. Brand new. Madison Beech wouldn't bother to have a car shipped out to her new house. She'd just buy one to leave here.

A very nice one.

"Earth to Andrea," Madison said, nudging her.

"Sorry!"

"I've been talking to you for at least a minute," Madison said. "I don't even really know where we're going, except that it's towards Connecticut."

Andrea laughed, then Madison told her how to say the address out loud so the onboard navigation system would plot their route.

"Good," Madison said, once they were following the nav's blue line. "Now, tell me what you were thinking about. Was it AJ?" she raised her eyebrows suggestively.

"Oh not at all," Andrea said. "It's this murder. I think I've figured something out, and we'll find out when we get to the gallery."

"Well, while you look for clues, I'm looking for art," Madison said. "And I feel a little naughty, because my designer really wanted to come out and shop with me, but I don't want to wait for him. I'm determined to make the Beach Hill house comfortable for *me*, not like some designer showplace." The words came out with a tinge of bitterness attached.

"Uh-huh," Andrea said with a grin. "Designer showplaces get old fast. I mean, I ditched that look *years* ago."

For a moment, confusion swept over Madison's face, then it broke into a wide smile. She laughed—a raucous cackle, not like the dainty chuckle Andrea expected. It made her laugh, too.

So many aspects of Madison's life were foreign to Andrea —her money and fame meant she moved in a completely different orbit most of the time—but there were times like this when it felt like they were more the same than different. Even though one of them was a pop star.

"Do you mind calling me Maddie when we're there?" Madison asked. She explained that she never used "Maddie" as part of her public, stage-based persona, bringing it out only when she was trying to keep a low profile. Andrea also realized Madison was "dressed down" for the excursion: tailored jeans, slip on hot pink sneakers, and an oversized faded blue Beach Hill hoodie that looked vaguely familiar.

"Is that my sweatshirt?" Andrea asked.

Madison nodded. "You left it at my place after movie night."

"I love that sweatshirt! You have a squillion dollars. Why are you wearing my ratty Beach Hill hoodie?"

"Because," Maddie said seriously, "No one expects me to."

Andrea wasn't sure if that was a compliment or not, but she didn't have time to ask. Madison parked in front of Well-Best. She peered in the rearview mirror, then twisted her long blond hair into a bun at the nape of her neck. She added oversized sunglasses and zipped the hoodie most of the way up. "How's that?" she asked, turning to Andrea.

"I'd never know it was you," Andrea deadpanned. Madison stuck out her tongue and they got out of the car. Not a paparazzo in sight.

"Let's spend some money," Madison said, pushing open the door.

… *and find a clue*, Andrea thought.

Janess met them at the door.

"Janess, this is my friend, Maddie," Andrea said, not knowing what last name to use.

Under her pink bangs, Janess's eyes narrowed. "Maddie," she repeated slowly.

"Maddie St. James," the pop star said easily. She kept her sunglasses on, but turned to regard the whole place. "I'm interested in some pieces to add to my employer's collection."

The ease with which she lied amazed Andrea. Madison's voice was steady and smooth, and she held herself with a different bearing—more languid, less bubbly and frenetic than what Andrea typically saw. Which was the "real" Madison? Not for the first time, Andrea reminded herself that she'd likely never know.

"Your… employer," Janess repeated, skepticism oozing off the word.

"Yes," Madison said crisply. "And I don't have a lot of time today, so if you'd like to earn a sizable commission, let's get to work."

Janess glanced at Andrea, but went straight into Gallery Director mode, leading them into the cavernous space. "We represent a specific selection of contemporary artists whose work is on the forefront of the current movements. From the incisive to the whimsical, we feel that WellBest galleries has the most—"

A wave of Maddie's hand cut her off. "What's that?"

The piece she was standing in front of was oversized—

Andrea estimated it had to be at least six feet tall—and comprising tiny dots of paint in cool blues, browns, and grays. To Andrea, it looked like the ocean sky before a storm.

Janess quoted the price, the five figures making Andrea want to faint, and Madison nodded. "We'll take that," she said. She turned to Andrea. "I think that will look beautiful over his mantel, don't you?"

Andrea could only nod.

"Alright, then. If you come over, we can do the—"

"I'm not finished yet," Madison said. She strode across the floor as though she were wearing three-inch stilettos, not canvas sneakers, and stopped in front of another large piece. "Tell me about this one."

Janess scurried to her, leaving Andrea to stand and marvel at the Madison's girl boss energy. After a moment, though, she remembered what she was there to look for.

"Restroom?" she called to the other women. Janess gave a nod and pointed upstairs.

Andrea bypassed the bathroom and went straight for the door marked "office." The police tape was down. Steve Jackman's stuff was a mess—some of it due to his untidiness, some undoubtedly from the police rifling through his belongings.

Andrea wasn't interested in any of the paperwork. She was here for the art.

Jackman's office was decorated in enormous black, white, and neon orange abstract paintings. The colors were enough to nearly give her a headache.

On the far left side of the room, hanging above the printer stand, was an out-of-place painting. Another garden-inspired landscape, impressionistic and all pastel colors.

It looked very similar to the one in Mike's shed.

Andrea crossed the room and carefully lifted the painting off the wall. Dwarfed by the other pieces in the room, it was a lot larger than it appeared. She placed it on the floor, leaning up against a filing cabinet, and took a closer look.

An unruly garden of flowers made up the foreground, a

white fence running about two-thirds of the way up the painting. In the distance, a pond added a sliver of blue, and the sky was a bleached-out periwinkle.

Pretty, Andrea thought. But definitely not something a modern art lover would hang on his wall. She turned the painting around. The frame looked the same as the one Mike unwrapped—plain back, a wire stretched taut across the back —brown paper covering it. She ran her hands around the edge of the frame, to see if the paper was loose or would come off. Nothing. Quickly, she grabbed a few pictures of the front and back of the painting with her phone, then hung it back on the wall.

To keep up appearances, she went into the bathroom, flushed the toilet, and washed her hands.

When she returned to the gallery, Janess and Madison were wrapping up the paperwork portion of the sale.

"Will the gallery deliver and hang the pieces?"

"Of course," Janess replied. They made arrangements. Andrea had to give her credit: She barely flinched when Madison gave her the address.

"It's been a pleasure."

"Thank you, Ms. St. James," Janess responded. "I hope your… ahem… *employer* enjoys them."

Madison didn't even give a backward glance, just a curt nod of the head and strode to the door. Andrea hustled to keep up.

"Thanks for opening for us," she said to Janess as they passed.

"No problem. Although your *friend* isn't fooling anyone." Janess emphasized the word, almost drawing air quotes around it.

"Oh?" A light sweat broke out on the back of Andrea's neck.

"The address gave it away. She's at the Rothkin estate. What is she, the granddaughter or something?"

Andrea found herself nodding. "She's trying to keep it

low-key," she said, stifling a laugh.

"I'm not gonna say a word to anyone."

Andrea smiled, but inside wondered if Janess was telling the truth.

"What took you so long?" Madison snapped as she got in the car. "I think she recognized me."

Andrea waved her off. "Easy there, Maddie St. James. She thinks you're Mrs. Rothkin's granddaughter. And, speaking of," she added, "What's up with the St. James, anyway?"

Maddie laughed, pulling the big car out of the space and onto the road. "It's the name of the street where I lived as a little kid," she said. "I have to use a fake name in a lot of places so I don't attract attention, and this is one I never forget."

"Of course. Well, while you were buying two—"

"Four."

"Four pieces of art. I did some sneaking upstairs." She quickly told Madison about finding the out-of-place painting and how it was similar to the one Mike Rimbeau had in his shed. "There's something there. I have to find out more about those paintings."

Madison nodded. "Maybe they're stolen?" she said.

Andrea considered the possibility. "Maybe," she said, "But I don't think an art dealer would display a stolen painting right on the wall of his office, no matter how private it is."

"How are you going to find out?"

Andrea pondered the question. "First step is to identify what they did with those paintings, then go from there."

Thinking about the paintings reminded her of Capt. Rimbeau, which in turn reminded her she was due to call the Beach Hill PD when she got back to her desk. She almost groaned out loud.

"When are those pieces being delivered?" she asked.

"Day after tomorrow." Maddie pulled into a drive thru

and ordered an iced latte, and Andrea a hot chocolate. Andrea took it gratefully, reminding herself not to carry the coffee chain's cup into Didi's shop. There'd be no cinnamon cardamom rolls for her if Di saw the orange and pink logo.

Madison dropped Andrea at her office with a promise to have her come up later, and pulled away.

Left alone, Andrea had no choice: She had to call the police.

CHAPTER 19

A maretto and Lemon greeted her at the Biscotti Realty office door, tails wagging. Even though they likely didn't need to go out, she took them anyway to put off making the phone call as long as possible.

The boys were grateful for the quick walk, but they were all back at the office a little too soon for Andrea's taste.

She sat at her desk, cracked her neck, and sighed.

Eat the frog, Andrea, she admonished herself. Maybe the police station would be closed? It *was* dinnertime. At least the thought made her chuckle.

Before she could avoid it again, she grabbed the phone and punched in the number.

"Beach Hill Police non-emergency line. How can I direct your call?" the deep voice on the other end said.

Even though she'd done nothing wrong except hiding evidence in her office refrigerator, Andrea's heart picked up speed and her palms got sweaty.

"Andrea Biscotti returning Niles the—Niles Needermey-er's call," she said, almost using Niles' childhood nickname.

"Please hold," the voice responded, and she slumped over her desk, phone in one hand, forehead in the other.

A click, a couple of rings later, and then, "Officer Needermeyer here," and a robotic voice cut in: "This call is being recorded."

"Recorded?" Andrea screeched.

"Easy there," Neddermeyer's nasal whine had changed little since they were in school together. "It's standard procedure."

Andrea didn't care if it was "standard procedure" or not—she didn't like it, and was instantly on guard. She waited.

"So, ahhh, nice to hear from you, Andrea," Needermeyer's mispronunciation of her name was made even more grating by his nasally voice.

This was not a social call, and Andrea was not about to act like it was. "You told me to call you," she said briskly. "And I am, and I have a mountain of work to do, so…."

"Understood. I am investigating the murder of Steve Jackman, and I understand you've been… asking questions." The contempt in his voice was clear.

"Is that a crime, Niles?" By the tiny puff of air he let out, she knew that Niles would have preferred her to use his title of officer. She didn't care.

"Well, to whom have you been speaking?"

Andrea rolled her eyes. "No one, really." She reminded herself that she was being recorded and stayed quiet.

"Do you expect me to believe that?" he asked after a moment.

"I don't know," she said. She sat straighter in her chair. She didn't want to reveal anything that might get Ricky in more trouble, so she figured her best bet was to not say much at all.

"Why are you avoiding the question?"

"I'm not. Beach Hill is small. It's Boat Parade week. I talk to lots of people in town, because I'm a realtor and I know everyone. People are talking about what happened," she snapped. "Is there something wrong with any of that?"

She could almost hear his frustration. There was no way he could ask her the pointed questions he clearly wanted to ask without revealing information that he likely wasn't supposed to share. And since Andrea had no intention of giving him any opening, they were at an impasse.

"I think there's more to this, Andrea, and you'll be hearing from me again."

Andrea rolled her eyes at the phone. "I look forward to it, Niles."

She hung up, letting out an expletive after the phone was back on its cradle. Amaretto gave her a dirty look from his spot in the corner.

"Next time *you* talk to Niles the Nosepicker," she said.

He yawned at her.

"Exactly."

She contacted the incoming renters for Boat Parade weekend and was just about to leave for the night and head to Madison's when her cell buzzed with a text from Gwen.

Something's not right w Ricky.

Andrea's heart dropped. The next text followed on the heels of the first.

Meet me at Front St beach—near Melville's nest

Be there in 5 she responded.

What was he up to now?

As soon as the dogs saw Gwennie, they pushed against her legs and demanded snuggles, as though they knew she was hurting. They always seemed to know exactly what people needed. Andrea hung back, holding on to the far end of their double leash, as Gwen crouched, cooed, and cuddled. When she straightened, Andrea came closer.

"Something's wrong," Gwennie said, lower lip quivering. "He took off this morning while it was still dark, and he had this big bag with him. I was up because I haven't been sleeping well, and I heard the apartment door open. When I went looked outside, he was getting in his car." The tears spilled over, running down her cheeks. "I've waited all day, but he hasn't come back. I'm afraid to call his cell in case the police are tracking it. I don't know what to do, or who to tell."

"Do you need to tell anyone?" Andrea asked, a rock of dread forming in her stomach.

"Niles Needermeyer told me to keep an eye on him, and I don't want to get in trouble."

Andrea fumed. That wasn't a fair position to put Gwen in, and Niles knew it. Gwen wasn't her brother's jailer.

"Forget the police for a second. What kind of bag was it? Do you think he's left town?"

"It was a dark duffel bag—the kind people take to the gym. I guess he could have put some clothes in there, but not many."

Andrea started. "What did you say?"

"I said, I guess he could have put some clothes in there, but not that many…"

"No, about the bag."

Gwennie stopped. "Oh. Well, it was about this big-" she spread her hands about two feet apart—"and this tall"—about eight inches.

A thrill of excitement shot through Andrea. "Was it gray?"

Gwennie closed her eyes as though visualizing the scene. "Hard to tell. It was just about dawn. But the bag was dark colored."

Andrea couldn't be one hundred percent sure, but from her cousin's description, it certainly sounded like the same bag that Steve Jackman had been carrying when he left his office the night of the murder.

And that wasn't good at all.

She couldn't tell her cousin, of course. But what to do with that information? Go to the police? Niles Needermeyer would love nothing more than for her to turn Ricky in for murder. But Andrea couldn't do that until she talked to Ricky and found out what was in that bag. And how those floral paintings fit in to everything.

"It doesn't sound like he took off," she said, lying almost as smoothly as Madison. "I bet he'll be back later. Will you text me when you see him?"

"What makes you say that?" Gwennie narrowed her eyes in suspicion. Amaretto, who'd been sniffing the sad at their feet with Lemon, gave a sharp bark. Andrea wasn't sure if this was in support of Gwen or not.

"Just… the bag seems small. He knows he's in trouble and running will make it worse, and it's been three days, so why run now? If he were going to take off, I'd think he would have done it sooner." The flimsy reasons came easily, and although they wouldn't have worked for Andrea, Gwen seemed eager to buy them.

She gave Andrea a big hug, which, considering she had the dog leash in one hand and a supremely guilty conscience, she accepted as gracefully as she could, giving Gwen a half-hearted pat on the back.

"I always feel better after talking to you," Gwen said. Andrea gave her a weak smile.

"I'm so glad," she said. But inside, all she was thinking was, *Is Ricky guilty?* And that did not make her feel better at all.

CHAPTER 20

Andrea closed up the office and walked the dogs home, thinking about her conversation with Gwen the whole time. The bag Ricky was carrying had to be the one that Janess saw Steve leaving with on Friday night.

And his hat was in her office fridge.

She fed the boys, gave them some attention, then texted Madison.

Get here! Im making tacos came the immediate response.

Andrea did not know what Madison's taco-making skills were, but she was starving and willing to find out.

In order to not show up empty-handed, she took the long way to Madison's, looping into Westshore to go to the big supermarket and grab some sides.

A blue truck, suspiciously like her cousin's, passed her as she waited to pull out of the market parking lot. The I'd rather be fishing sticker on the back confirmed it. She cut two people off pulling out of the lot, but didn't care.

She followed Ricky down Route 1. It seemed he was headed back into Beach Hill. He was coming south, so he could have been in any of two dozen places between Beach Hill and Providence.

He turned towards town, and she followed him right to his driveway, giving a friendly honk as he exited his truck.

She parked across the bottom of his driveway, blocking him in.

Like that matters. He's already been wherever he was going. Still, it felt like a very Solving Mystery thing to do.

Andrea got out of her car and leaned against it. Ricky, wearing a pair of beat up jeans and a Sox tee, closed the door of his truck.

"You following me?" he asked.

Andrea's heart kicked it up a notch. "Well, I mean, I saw you when I was leaving the market. Nice to see you, too," she said, faking her way through the exchange.

Ricky grunted.

Andrea tried honesty. "Look, Gwen was worried when she didn't see you around today," she said—leaving out the whole bit about Gwen actually seeing him leave. "And I found out some stuff about Steve Jackman that I wanted to talk with you about, so I figured I'd take advantage and see if I could get you."

Ricky just scowled.

"I know Jackman had a partner named Riggs, and when he left his office on Friday night he was carrying something in a bag. Do you know who Riggs is? Do you know what was in the bag?"

Ricky gaped at her. He closed his mouth, then took three big steps down the driveway and was right in front of her.

"I don't know how to make myself more clear," he said in a low voice. "But you need. To. Stop. Messing. Around." The last bit came out through gritted teeth. "This is serious."

Andrea was not about to back down this time. "I *know* it's serious. I was on the phone with Niles Needermeyer a little while ago. And I know you know what was in Jackman's bag." She said everything evenly and quietly, holding a level gaze.

Ricky's face went white, then red. "Are you *kidding me?*" he cried, voice raised. "What is wrong with you? You have *no idea* who you're dealing with! How did you even know about the bag?" He was breathing heavily; Andrea could see the effort it took to keep himself under control.

"I'm dealing with you, cousin," Andrea said. "And with Mike Rimbeau, who's maybe down at the station, if Niles digs too deep. So if you know anything, you should think about telling me."

Ricky threw his arms up and rubbed his head. "Not here," he growled, and tugged her toward his porch.

She followed him into the darkness of the enclosed porch. At this time of night, there was a chill in there. She rubbed her upper arms. Ricky got low and close to her ear.

"Look, the bag was for a delivery to his partner. A… payment. It's taken care of. That's all you need to know. And don't go telling Needermeyer."

Andrea ignored the last part and crossed her arms. "Payment, what for? How much was in the bag?"

"Enough. Enough for me to take care of things." He turned away from her. "And I'd do it again, too," he muttered.

An icy wave came over Andrea. Had he really just said that? Was that a confession?

He threw open the door to the apartment, turned his head, and tossed a "goodbye, Andrea," over his shoulder. In an instant, the door was closed and he was gone.

The chill from the porch followed her outside.

Had Ricky just confessed to murder?

It sure sounded like it.

She walked to her car, numb, questions whipping through her head like a tornado: What had he done? What had he meant? What "things" had he taken care of? He knew who Riggs was. Why wouldn't he turn him in?

No matter what the answers turned out to be, none would be good.

She opened her car door to the insistent buzzing, momentarily breaking her from her spiraling thoughts.

Thinking it was Madison, she planned to send the call directly to voicemail. Instead, there was an unfamiliar number and multiple missed calls. What now?

"Andrea Biscotti?" A voice she didn't recognize bit at her name like they were chewing ice.

"Yes?" She struggled to get her churning insides under control.

"It's Flavia Bunco," the caller said.

Flavia who?

The caller gave a short laugh. "Of course you've forgotten. Bunco. My family is renting one of your—"

OH NO!

It was as if a bucket of ice water was poured over her head.

"Cottage seven," she said quickly. "Yes; I know. I'm so sorry I'm late. There was a family emergency. I'll be there in five minutes." She started the car, hands shaking, and pulled out into the street.

How had she forgotten that the Buncos asked for an early check-in for the boat parade? She wanted to bang her head on the steering wheel, but instead flew as fast as she could down to Front Street and the office.

Well, she knew *how* she'd forgotten: She'd been so caught up in the Ricky situation she'd neglected everything else—like her actual job.

She raced in, grabbed the orange plastic key stamped with Beach Hill Cottages and a big "7", fished an emergency gift card to Didi's out of her top drawer, and raced across the street to the beach. She moved along as fast as she could without all-out sprinting and looking even more like a disaster, choosing instead to speed walk.

A blond-haired woman in a sleek black dress and sunhat that would cast a shadow bigger than Jupiter stood in the darkness outside of Cabin 7.

"I'm so sorry, Mrs. Bunco," she said. "We have been dealing with a family emergency this week, and as you know we are a small operation. I am deeply sorry." She fished in her pocket for the gift card. "Here's a token to show you how much I appreciate your patience." As she extended the gift card, she deftly inserted the key in the lock, twisting the knob and opening the cottage.

Thankfully, the place was immaculate.

Andrea's heart slowed. "Can I show you and your family around?"

Mrs. Bunco gave a brittle smile. "My husband took the children to get some ice cream while we waited, but you can show me whatever you need to."

Andrea gave her the quick tour: TV remote, pots and pans, linens, and told her where to stake out the best spot for viewing the boat parade over the weekend. By the time she was done with her tour, Mrs. Bunco's smile was less brittle and more genuine, and Andrea felt a little better.

"If you need anything, please reach out," she finished.

"Absolutely," Mrs. Bunco said. Two boys wearing matching polo shirts and a gentleman in a Yankees cap appeared at the door.

"We good to go?" the man, who Andrea assumed was Mr. Bunco, asked.

"All good. Miss Biscotti here even gave us a gift card for our trouble."

"It's for the tea shop across from Front Street Park." She pointed at Didi's bright pink awning. "Can't miss it."

They said their goodbyes and Andrea walked back to her car, more slowly this time.

She fairly collapsed when she climbed in. With everything that had been going on with Ricky, and now this, Andrea didn't even know herself. She had *never* missed a check-in, and little did Mrs. Bunco know that new arrivals typically received a basket of candy, a map, and other treats. She'd have to deliver one tomorrow at some point. To ensure she remembered, she set an alarm on her phone.

And then came the message from Madison.

TACOS. Where r u???

Andrea dropped her head to the steering wheel and groaned. She sat in the car, trying to sort through her emotions. Her life was going out of control. How had this happened? A few weeks ago, she wasn't involved in a murder investigation, didn't have a friend who was a pop star, and remembered when each of her guests was due to check in.

And didn't have a cute guy interested in her.

And didn't have much of a life, to be honest.

Fair.

Still, there had to be a happy medium, right?

The phone buzzed angrily. Madison sent a GIF of tacos falling from the sky.

Andrea shook her head.

Her existential crisis had to be put on hold for the time being, evidently.

CHAPTER 21

B y the time she pulled up to the Rothkin gate (when would she think of it as "Madison's gate"?), she had herself a little more together, although the possibility of Ricky's guilt still ate away at her.

Had he actually killed Steve Jackman? How big was the payoff the bag contained? What should she do with the hat? What role did he have in all this?

She still wrestled with those questions as she grabbed the bag from the market and headed toward Madison's door.

She buzzed.

"Come in!" Madison's singsong voice came over the intercom and the door buzzed, unlocked.

That's new, Andrea thought.

She let herself in and carried her grocery bag to the kitchen at the back of the house. "How'd you know it was me?" she asked, putting the bag down. She emptied its contents onto the island: Mild salsa, tortillas, hot salsa, chips, and guacamole.

"You brought tortillas!" Madison screeched. She was wearing a toile apron with a black bow on the front pocket that looked as though it belonged on store mannequin, not in a real kitchen. She rushed around the piano-shaped island and gave Andrea a big hug.

"Can't have tacos without tortillas," Andrea said.

"How'd you know I'd forget the tortillas?" Madison asked. Andrea just raised an eyebrow.

On the stove was a cast-iron skillet, sizzling with peppers and onions. Black beans simmered in a pot at the back. Andrea rubbed her arms.

"I'm impressed," Andrea said. "And chilly."

"It's the one thing I can make," Madison admitted. "Not for nothing, but I'm starving. I called you *eons* ago." While Madison emoted, she grabbed paper plates and scooped some veggies onto one. "Close the door? I had it open in case of a cooking emergency. Pull it hard—it sticks," she added, as Andrea struggled.

"Evidently." Andrea gave the door a tremendous yank to close it, then filled Madison in as she made her own pate. Madison didn't take a tortilla or guac, but loaded up on the veggies and salsa.

"I'm carb-free," she said apologetically when she saw Andrea looking at her plate. "Photo shoot next week."

Andrea rolled her eyes. "Life is too short not to eat carbs." She took an extra tortilla, because today she sure needed some.

Madison shrugged. "Hey, not related to carbs at all, I was wondering if you wouldn't mind being here to meet the art. Yanno, since you have so much free time solving mysteries and all."

Andrea worked really hard not to groan. "Ask me tomorrow? Right now, I am really wishing you bought more carbs and cheese, because eating my feelings with veggies alone is not satisfying."

"Fair enough." Madison scooped another pile of veggies. "And you're right. Cheese would be way better."

. . .

It was after nine by the time Andrea finally got home for the night. She was bone-tired, but the dogs needed to go out. She also needed to do some laundry, too, but *that* wasn't going to happen.

By the time she collapsed into bed, she was sure her head would hit the pillow and she'd go right to sleep.

Two hours later: No such luck. All that her tossing and turning earned her was dirty looks from the dogs and the start of an epic headache.

She threw off the covers and trudged into the kitchen. Warm milk? Gross in anything but the depth of winter. Instead, she grabbed the jar of peanut butter, a butter knife, and a banana, got the unicorn notebook, and sat at the table.

First, she peeled the entire banana. Then she cut it lengthwise, to make two long pieces. Methodically, she spread the peanut butter on one half of the banana. She put the other half on top, then bisected the pieces. Voila! Two peanut butter and banana "sandwiches."

As she worked her way through the gooey treat, she added to the list in her notebook:

- Steve's business was in Connecticut, but he had a boat slip in Beach Hill
- Steve got a call and left the gallery on Friday night to head to the boat. (From "Riggs")
- The boat was lit up during Uncle Eddie's party
- Jackman had a dark gray bag with him—a payoff to Riggs
- Ricky was on the boat to help fix the bilge pump with Ratchet Bob
- Capt. Mike Rimbeau was also on the boat
- Ratchet Bob and Capt. Mike left, and Ricky was still on the boat with Steve
- Somehow Ricky ended up with Jackman's bag
- Andrea had Ricky's SeaDogs hat in her refrigerator

- Janess had said Steve was a jerk to work for
- Jackman's body had been found in the cove the next morning
- Ricky delivered the money to Riggs

No matter how she twisted the facts, or which way she looked at things, she kept coming up with the same answer: Ricky was guilty.

Ricky's a murderer.

The thought echoed around and around her head. Her stomach clenched, the PB & banana sandwich rolling in there. She'd have to go to the police and tell them what she knew, right? Otherwise, she'd be some sort of accessory? Or arrested for withholding information?

That made her feel even worse.

But, even though everything she knew pointed to *guilty*, she still couldn't reconcile any of it with the kid she'd grown up with, the cousin who worked for her, or the son who took his mom to the specialty fish market once a week.

It just doesn't make sense.

Andrea tapped the pen against her teeth. There was something there she couldn't see, a missing piece she had to identify.

Maybe I should sleep on it, she thought. Her mom always said that was the best way to work through a puzzle. Provided you *could* sleep.

She looked at the clock: it was nearly two-thirty. Tomorrow—later—she had to deliver a basket to the Buncos, reach out to AJ, since he'd sent her a few texts and she hadn't responded, and—oh yeah—probably go to the police with her ideas about the murder. Good times.

She left her notebook and pen on the table, put her peanut butter knife in the sink, and wandered back to her room. From his bed on the floor, Limoncello peeked out from under half-open lids and gave one thump with his tail, while Amaretto had taken the opportunity to plant himself smack in the middle of her bed while she was gone. Stretched out, laying on his side, he looked twice his normal size.

Andrea sighed, then carefully climbed under the covers so as not to disturb him. Although she had to scrunch on the edge of the bed, this time her brain let her body settle.

Thank goodness, she thought, just before the wave of sleep overtook her.

As Andrea staggered through her morning, she reflected that if this were a movie, she'd have a perfectly formed solution to the mystery of who killed Steve Jackman that completely exonerated her cousin the minute she opened her eyes.

But instead, she spilled the milk when making her hot chocolate; the dogs wanted to go for an extra-long beach walk to punish her for her recent absences, and since she hadn't done laundry, she had to wear her last resort wedgie-inducing undies, meaning she'd be uncomfortable all day long.

And she still didn't know who the murder was.

She tossed her stuff in her bag, clicked the boys to their leash, adjusted her undies, and opened the door to her apartment.

It hit her with the salt air.

The fish market! The fish market that Ricky always took his mom to on Saturday mornings! *That* was it!

The dogs sensed her enthusiasm and raced her to the driveway. She'd planned on walking them to work, but opened the car door instead.

Why hadn't I thought of the market earlier?

She laughed out loud a little climbing into the car, amazed that she'd missed something so obvious.

When she got behind the wheel, she wasn't entirely sure where to go first: To the police station? Or down to the Shore Shack?

She drummed her fingers on the steering wheel. She *could* go straight to Niles, but her theory would require her to convince him of a few things. If she went to the Shore Shack first, she could likely bring him more concrete evidence.

The Shore Shack it was, then!

CHAPTER 22

On the short drive into town, she figured out her plan. It made so much sense, really: The fish market set up early Saturday mornings—like three AM, early—so the fishermen could come straight in and unload their wares. They organized and filled restaurant orders first, then were open to the public around six, six-thirty.

Ricky had texted Gwen a little after midnight, asking him to meet her behind the Sip 'n Scoop. There was no way Gwen could've met him there, not only because she was annoyed at his behavior at the party, but because the *back of the Sip 'n Scoop was where they kept all the stuff needed to set up for the fish market!*

The message wasn't a request; it was a code.

If Gwen couldn't actually meet Ricky in the place where he said he was going to be, that meant there was something else he wanted her to do when and if she came there.

And Andrea *knew* it had to do with that bag.

The Captain was in.

Andrea walked the dogs across the parking lot to the Shore Shack, taking her time, formulating her questions. She needed to get just the right info out of Capt. Mike without making him suspicious.

Before she got to his door, however, he emerged and gave her a wave.

"Ahoy!" he called.

She waved back and nudged the dogs more quickly in his direction.

"The police are calling me," she said instead of a greeting.

Capt. Mike gave her a funny look. "I bet," he said, stretching his bad leg. "Needermeyer's been down here a lot, asking questions."

"Are you going to tell him about the package?" Andrea said.

"You got something you want to say to me? Or are you just gonna keep trying to boss me around?" Capt. Mike said sharply, "'cause I have stuff to do today. Boat parade's this weekend and it's a busy time."

Andrea ignored his question, but let the dogs sniff Capt. Mike's shoes. "Is the fish market open this weekend?" she asked instead.

Mike seemed off-kilter, like that was the last thing he'd expected her to ask—and he seemed a little sheepish after speaking gruffly a moment before.

"Sure it is," he said. "Every Saturday, rain or shine, May first 'til October fifteen or thereabouts."

"And they're still storing the set-up materials behind the Sip 'n Scoop?"

Mike nodded slowly, like he was trying to figure out where she was going with this, and why, after living in Beach Hill her whole life, she was asking him these questions.

Amaretto pulled at the leash, tugging towards Melville, the one-legged seagull, who hopped along the pier. A pair of sunglasses dangled from his beak. Andrea considered her next statement carefully.

"So why would Ricky be texting his sister to meet him behind the Sip 'n Scoop on a Friday night?"

Mike furrowed his brow. "I don't know. Seems weird to me."

"Sure does. Because he wasn't texting *her*."

"You've lost me," said Capt. Mike. But Andrea watched his eyes, which darted down and to the side, like he was planning his escape route.

"Ricky texted Gwen by *mistake*," she said, a note of triumph creeping into her voice. "It was *you* who he wanted to meet, not her. He had Steve Jackman's bag and knew that you were the next person in the chain who needed it.

"But you never got it, did you? Because *you* didn't get the message. So you've been holding on to the painting this whole time, but Riggs—whomever he is—got ticked off, because you didn't have his payment. Am I right?" It all came out in a rush, and Andrea was pretty proud of herself for putting the pieces together: Jackman and the mysterious Riggs were smuggling paintings through Captain Mike, to go… somewhere. And Ricky ended up in the wrong place at the wrong time and took the bag from the boat. Riggs must have also been on the boat and killed Jackman—maybe because Ricky took the bag? Or they argued? Anyway, that part wasn't for her to figure out. But it seemed to Andrea that Riggs was likely the person who killed Jackman once everyone left the boat.

The transformation that came over Capt. Mike's face was unexpected: It went from bright and cheerful, to furrowed brows and storm clouds gathering in his blue eyes. If Andrea hadn't been in the middle of town, she'd likely be more scared than she was.

"You think you've figured it out, don't you?" he growled. "You don't know anything." Mike took a menacing step closer, and Lemon and Amaretto instantly planted themselves in front of her, eyes narrowed, hackles raised, growls rumbling low in their chests. She had never seen that behavior from the boys and was more surprised by them than by Capt. Mike. They made her brave.

"I know enough."

She clicked her tongue and the boys immediately tuned away with her, heading towards her car.

I guess I made him suspicious, after all.

She fought the urge to giggle and held her head high.... feeling Capt. Mike's eyes bore into her back the whole time.

Capt. Mike's reaction confirmed a few things for Andrea: one, the message had not been intended for Gwennie, and two, that Capt. Mike was more involved in this fiasco than their initial conversation seemed.

But it still didn't quite exonerate Ricky for Steve Jackman's murder.

She needed a little more information, after all, before going to the police.

Andrea parked the car up Front Street and brought the dogs to the Biscotti Realty Office. She had to put together and deliver that basket for the Bunco family, and now seemed like the right time to tackle that project.

There was a stash of white wicker baskets in the Biscotti Realty supply closet. She grabbed one and a blue and white checked napkin to line it. She added the candy, water bottles and a beach ball for the kids to toss around. All that was left was a trip to Didi's for some cinnamon rolls.

She left the basket and the boys in the office and headed down the street.

"Hello, stranger," Didi said as soon as the bell tinkled. The morning rush was over, but it was still early enough in the season that there was a lull before lunch. The cafe was empty.

"Tell me about it." Andrea slid onto a stool at the counter and leaned on the cool marble. "It's been crazy."

Didi finished steaming the milk for her hot chocolate, added a squirt of whipped cream, and slid the mug to her. "Wanna tell me about it?"

Andrea filled her in as quickly as possible, bringing her through the paintings on the wall and in the shed, Capt. Rimbeau and Riggs, the bag, and the mistaken message from Ricky. She even added in the dogs' bravery.

By the time she finished talking, her hot chocolate was half empty and Didi was leaning over her side of the counter. "Sounds to me like someone better keep an eye on Mike Rimbeau."

Andrea nodded. "I've gotta deliver a check-in basket, get the rest of rentals squared away, and swing by Madison's so I can get the openers or keys or whatever she's using so I can meet the art tomorrow."

Didi gave her an impish grin. "I wasn't talking about *you* monitoring him." She gestured to the cafe and out its huge front window, which overlooked Front Street Park, the docks, and the Shore Shack. "Boo and I've got this."

"Really?" The wave of relief coursing through Andrea's body was palpable and unexpected. She hadn't realized how stressed she was.

"Of course," Didi giggled, tossing her blond bob. "I am an exceptional spy, and Boo is going to prep the smoker for Boat Parade weekend, so he'll be outside and able to watch things, too. Won't you, honey?" She called the last part out to ensure Boo could hear. Clacking tongs from the kitchen signaled Boo's agreement.

"You're the best," Andrea said. She reached across the counter and gave her friend's arm a squeeze. "Seriously." She paused. "I also seriously need some cinnamon rolls for that check-in basket."

"I gotchu." Didi disappeared, and Andrea spun on her stool to look out the window. There were more cars on Front Street today, in anticipation of the parade this weekend. A few shoppers meandered from store to store across the street at the collection known as The Point. The seagulls whirled overhead, and the docked boats bobbed in place. All of it—the view, the atmosphere, even the way the air smelled—was as familiar to Andrea as her own reflection.

But she was coming to realize that familiar only went so deep, and what was underneath her familiar life was a lot more complicated than she'd ever known.

CHAPTER 23

The Buncos, delighted with their basket, and especially the two extra cinnamon cardamom rolls that Didi had thrown in, had completely forgiven Andrea for her previous day's mistake. They were headed to explore the beach and the local lighthouse, and, after giving them some suggestions on where to go for dinner, she left, satisfied that her customer relations record would remain top-notch and there'd be no disgruntled online reviews.

But every other cottage was due to fill over the next couple of days, so she whipped through each one, fluffing towels, ensuring there were soaps and pot lids and precisely made beds, wishing Ricky was available to help her out.

He should be able to come back to work, she grumbled to herself, finishing up in Cottage twelve. It took her longer than she'd expected to get through all the other rentals, and now she was hot, sweaty, and annoyed.

And she had to go back to the office and get the rest of the check-ins organized.

As she trudged across the parking lot from the cottages to Front St, she risked a peek behind her sunglasses toward the Shore Shack.

The Captain was not in. Probably for the first time Andrea

could remember, the sign was flipped over. Heart sinking, she texted Di.

Capt. is OUT. See anything?

The text came back a moment later.

Sign flipped, but he's in the shack. Has come out the back 2x.

Di was on it. Relieved, sent a thumbs up and tucked her phone in her pocket, continuing across the parking lot.

The boys clamored for a walk when she got back to the office. "Just a quick one," she said, taking them away from the beach, up the steps behind the office to the tourist parking lot off Driftwood. She hadn't been up there since the morning after the murder. It felt like forever ago. She steered the boys to a clump of grass facing Front Street.

Ricky wanted to meet Capt. Mike behind the Sip 'n Scoop to give him the bag late Friday night, so Mike could give it to Riggs. Which meant Ricky didn't know Riggs—so how could he have met him yesterday? How did he get in touch with him? Captain Mike?

The spring sun warmed the top of Andrea's head. She hoped it would give her brain extra computing power.

The boys tugged her to the stairs. As she made her way to the Biscotti Realty office, she realized it wasn't about Riggs at all: Everything hinged on Captain Mike.

By the time she finished cleaning up, then checking all the guests into their rentals for the parade, Andrea was wiped. The lack of sleep caught up to her. She felt as though she'd been beaten all over her body with a tiny hammer.

There'd been a small rush at the end, as Cabins two, five, and six arrived for check in at the same time. Andrea slumped in her office chair, staring at the wall, willing energy to come back into her body.

Her phone buzzed.

She hadn't had a chance to look at it in about forty minutes.

Uh-oh.

Five missed texts. Four from Didi, one from Madison.

She opened Didi's first:

- 2:41pm CM taking something out of the shed. Wrapped in brown paper

- 2:43pm CM loading package into his truck

- 2:45pm CM leaving. What should we do??

- 2:47pm Boo following.

Yes! Di and Boo were, indeed, super spies. Captain Mike would never expect Boo to follow him. She tapped out a quick note of thanks and asked them to update her on where he landed.

Then she turned to Madison's message.

Surprise media project mtng in NYC. Left openers, etc w AJ. Don't forget!

As if she could. Or would. But ugh, now she had to work in catching up with AJ today, too.

Do you even hear *yourself?* The voice in her head nearly shouted at her. *What is* wrong *with you, girl?!*

Nothing wrong with meeting up with handsome AJ to get the keys to Madison's house, to let in the local gallery director in to hang Madison's expensive art tomorrow. Nothing wrong with that, at all. She took a breath, rubbed her eyes. The dogs, splayed out on their beds, also looked exhausted.

The text from Boo came as she was getting in the car to head to Madison's to meet AJ.

Capt Mike paying a visit to an ahht gallery. A photo followed.

When the pic came through, it did not surprise Andrea in the least. She thanked Boo and told him he was off duty. Then she sent a text of her own to AJ, to let him know she was coming up to the estate to get the keys.

And I have a job for you, she added.

. . .

AJ buzzed her in to Madison's place. There were fewer construction crews today, so the sound of saws and hammering from the far reaches of the house were at a minimum.

"Hey," AJ said, meeting her in the foyer. His hair was slicked—wet?—and he wore a blue and white checked button-down shirt that immediately made Andrea think of the welcome baskets she left for her the cottage guests, but not in a bad way.

She realized he was still waiting for her to answer.

"Hey!" she said, with way more enthusiasm than he had. Suddenly, things felt awkward between them. When had they kissed? Only a couple of days ago. Now she was as shy as a teen with her first crush.

"How's the investigation going?" They were still standing in the foyer, weirdly.

"Um, there's a lot happening," she said. "And I need your help with something, if that's okay. And the remotes to get into this house for tomorrow."

"Sure thing, All Business. I get it." AJ gave her a snappy salute.

Andrea's cheeks went hot.

"Sorry. I'm just fried and exhausted and..."

"And that's why it's amazing that you have a super-rich friend with a patio and fully stocked fridge and bar at your disposal." With that, AJ ushered her through the house, out the double set of French doors onto the patio, and pointed her to an oversized half-moon lounge chair. "Have a seat. Are the dogs in the car?" Andrea nodded. Her car keys were still in her hand. He plucked them from her, brushed her knuckles in a quick kiss, tossed a "don't move" over his shoulder, and disappeared back into the house.

Andrea couldn't move if she wanted to. She sunk into the lounger pillows and took a deep breath. Her brain knew she had to deal with the info she'd received from Boo, go over the final checklist for the cottage guests arriving the next day, and talk with her cousin, but her body just couldn't function anymore. Eyelids heavy, sun warm on her legs, Andrea let herself get swept into sleep.

CHAPTER 24

T he good news: the sun was still up when she woke. A blanket covered her legs. The bad news: she had no idea where she was. After a blinking, confused few moments, it all came back to her: Madison's patio, AJ, the dogs...

The dogs!

She scrambled out of the lounger—awkwardly, because it was big and the pillows were *so* soft—and whistled for her boys.

"Lemon! Amaretto!" Another whistle.

Their paws clacked on the hardwood. Andrea turned to the French doors and stepped into Madison's house. The dogs flew at her, AJ a couple of steps behind.

"Hey there!" he said. "I kept them inside because I was afraid they'd jump up and wake you. You were pretty much dead to the world by the time I brought them back from the car."

Andrea finished giving the boys their attention and stood. "How long was I out for?"

AJ grinned. "About an hour and a half. No offense, but you seemed like you needed it."

Andrea hoped she didn't snore, but didn't dare ask. They made their way to the kitchen, where AJ had set out the salsa from the previous night and a bag of tortilla chips—clearly not from Madison's pantry.

They scooped and munched.

"None taken. I did. And if I could, I would go back out there and crash again."

"But," AJ began.

"But I have a ton of stuff to do. Thank you for taking care of the guys for me." Andrea crunched a chip. Salsa dribbled on her chin, and AJ dabbed it with a napkin.

"Classy," Andrea muttered.

"No problem. You… said you had a job for me?" he reminded her.

Andrea nodded.

"I do. I'm wondering if you can set up a camera at the Shore Shack? I need some concrete evidence."

AJ raised one eyebrow, and Andrea's knees went a little weak. "That's… not exactly kosher."

"Is it illegal?"

"Not technically," he said. "But it's not, like… the greatest human thing to do."

Andrea considered this. "I don't think Mike is the greatest human," she pointed out. "But it may also be the way we make sure that Ricky is innocent."

They ate some chips in silence. AJ sighed and ran his hands through his hair.

"Fine. But I can't do it with any of my equipment—or Madison's."

"Sure, whatever you need," Andrea said. "No problem."

"I'll go tomorrow to get the stuff. I was going to ask you if you wanted to have dinner with me tonight, but…"

But, indeed. Even with the nap, Andrea realized how exhausted she was. And she wasn't lying—she had a ton to do. Plus, laundry. The wedgie problem was no joke.

"Rain check?"

"Of course." AJ gave her the gate remote and the new code to get into the house.

"It's a brand-new security system," he said, showing her the outside panel. "The company wants Madison to be their spokesperson. There are a few bugs to work out—one with the router, especially—but she wants to give it a go, so…" He shrugged.

"If Madison says yes, it happens," Andrea said.

"Pretty much."

He had her run through it twice to be sure she could get the door open. "Just call me if there are any hiccups," he said.

"Not that I can get cell service here," Andrea laughed. Madison's house was made of so much brick it was nearly impossible to get a signal in the house.

"Not a problem," AJ said. He showed Andrea how to switch her phone to a Wi-Fi calling mode, where the phone would hook up to Madison's internet. "No cell bars needed."

"Sweet." With all of that taken care of, there really were no more reasons to stay. Plus, even though Lemon and Amaretto enjoyed snuffling up the dropped bits of chips and salsa, they needed their own dinner.

AJ walked them all to the car, holding the dogs' leash. They obediently hopped into the back seat.

"Once you solve this mystery, Nancy Drew, we're going to dinner."

"Deal," she said, nerves tingling. He leaned in and gave her a light kiss, sending shocks through her body.

"Stupid murder," she muttered as she pulled out of the driveway. "Getting in the way of my love life." From the back seat, Amaretto woofed in agreement.

CHAPTER 25

The next morning, with her laundry done, undies replaced, dogs fed and walked on their normal schedule, and check-ins organized to her usual level of satisfaction, Andrea felt like a new person.

The nap and a good night's sleep helped, too.

Once the last of her guests checked in, she walked the dogs and got ready to meet Janess at Madison's.

"I'd take you, but I'm afraid you'll get in the way," she said to them. Limoncello gave her a reproachful look, like he'd never get underfoot and didn't know what she was talking about.

She opted to leave them at Biscotti Realty, figuring she'd swing back after the art was installed, pick them up, and check in with AJ. Maybe they'd be able to get dinner and go to the police together.

That's a great second date, right there.

What she *really* wanted was to stop in to Didi's for a quick chat session and a hot chocolate, but glancing at her watch she was afraid that she'd be late for Janess, so she headed straight up the hill to the Rothkin Estate on Daisy.

The gate opener worked, and she carefully punched in the code on the new security system.

DOOR ERROR blinked on the screen.

AJ told her she had three tries to get it right before the police were notified, and Andrea did *not* want to have to explain herself to them.

Especially not if Niles showed up.

She took a breath, checked the code on her phone, waited for the screen to set itself to the READY position, and tried again.

ACCESS GRANTED appeared. There was a buzz from the door, and the panel lit up green. Before it locked itself again, Andrea grasped the latch and let herself in. She went to send AJ a triumphant text, but had no cell signal or Wi-Fi connection. Yesterday he said something about a "router problem" with the new system—this seemed like a pretty big problem to have.

Oh well. Once the art was in, she'd be able to text him from the street.

She checked her watch. Janess and the crew to hang the pieces were due to arrive in fifteen minutes. Before they arrived, she placed sticky notes in each of the four places where Madison wanted the work hung, identifying which piece went where. The last thing she wanted was someone to put the wrong painting in the wrong room.

Task completed, she opened the French door to the luscious patio where she'd napped. She inhaled the tang of salt air—a smell that she'd grown up with her whole life and could never tire of. But yesterday she'd been so wiped she hadn't taken in the view: Rolling green lawn bordered by a tangled thicket of sea roses which would bloom later this summer. A weathered staircase, recently painted white, headed down to the private beach. Andrea couldn't see it from the patio. But she *could* see the Atlantic, glittering and blue, stretching all the way to the horizon.

Another stellar day. The weather was supposed to continue like this right through the Boat Parade, which would surely put it in the top ten of Andrea's lifetime.

Behind her, the door buzzed.

Here we go, she thought. *Let's get this done.* She'd stop by Didi's after for that hot chocolate.

When she opened the door, she was confused. Captain Mike stood there, not Janess.

"Um, hi?" she said. She was so caught off guard, when he moved to step in, she moved right out of the way and he entered the foyer. It was only when he closed the door with a loud-sounding *click!* that she noticed the roll of duct tape looped around one forearm.

"Where's Janess?" she got out, taking a step away from him. Her brain saw Capt. Mike, the friendly guy she'd known forever, but her body vibrated with adrenaline; her heart slamming against her ribs painfully. She was sure her hands were shaking.

"She's not coming." They were the first words he'd spoken, and the tone he used was flat and dark.

Andrea took another step back, and—quick as a striking snake—Capt Mike grabbed her forearm with one strong hand. "Easy there. You're staying with me."

"I… don't know what you want." Andrea forced the words out between breathy gasps of panic.

"I *want* you to come with me." Capt. Mike tightened his hold. Andrea winced. He tugged her into the back of the house, to the kitchen and its piano-shaped island. Using his foot, he dragged a chair away from the island and to the center of the room, all while holding her arm above her head so she was almost on tip-toe. She swung at him with her free hand, but she was off balance and it did no good. He backed her into the chair, forcing her to sit. The duct tape came off his arm, and he wrapped her ankles to the chair rungs and her wrists together behind her back in an instant.

Andrea tried to take some deep breaths, to get panic under control.

Breathe in. Breathe out, she told herself. *Breathe.*

Breathing was… not simple right now.

Captain Mike came out from behind the chair where he'd been taping her wrists to its back. He leaned against the island and crossed his arms.

"All right," he said. "Let's get down to business."

CHAPTER 26

A ndrea gulped. She couldn't believe she was a prisoner in
Madison Beech's kitchen.

"I-I don't understand. I really don't know what you're
doing here."

Capt. Mike—it was hard to think of him as anything other
than Captain Mike, even though he'd taped her to a chair—
scowled. "You asked way too many questions," he said.

"You were the one holding paintings and getting cash!"
Andrea said before she could stop herself. "And up until about
ten minutes ago I thought you were just a middleman."

He gave her a rueful smile. "Not exactly. You had that guy
from the coffee shop—the one who never says anything—
follow me yesterday."

"Tea shop," Andrea corrected automatically. "Didi's is a
tea shop."

"Whatever." He slammed an open hand on the counter-
top. "I don't care what it's called, that big guy was watchin'
me."

"What does that have to do with me?" Andrea cried. "Or
Steve Jackman or the art?"

"You're nosing around, trying to make sure your dear old
cousin doesn't go up for murder." Capt. Mike made his voice

high-pitched and mocking at the end, like not wanting an innocent family member to go to prison was a bad thing.

Andrea decided not to dignify that with a response.

Her brain raced: How could she get out of this? Her phone was in her pocket, but there was no cell service here. AJ knew where she was, presumably, but he was running errands in Windshore and she had no idea when he'd be back or if he'd even come here. Madison was in New York. Didi had no idea she was here.

Her heart sank. She'd have to figure her own way out of this mess… and that was looking pretty difficult.

Get him to talk, she thought. *Buy time for… something.*

She cleared her dry-as-a-sock throat.

"So there is no partner named Riggs," she started, hoping that would get him going.

Capt. Mike cackled. "No siree!"

Who *was* this guy? Certainly not the patient captain who taught Andrea to hoist a sail and tie a boat to a cleat.

"What *happened* to you?" she blurted. "This isn't like you."

Capt. Mike cocked his head at her. "You think you know me? You think you know me, just because I give the little brats in this town sailing lessons? I *hate* doing it. But I have to. I can't get by, otherwise. I've been paying off some debts to some not-so-great people. And when Steve Jackman and his big boat and his money came along, I was hoping to get out of water babysitting for good. Get out of *here* for good. Be done."

His words stung. Andrea filed some of the information away and moved on. "What did Steve Jackman have to do with it?"

Mike grabbed an apple from the bowl on the island and took a giant bite. "Steve was my way out," he said. "Had his gallery, but that was a loser. His money-maker on the side was forgeries. Expert fakes of famous Impressionist paintings that we'd sell to private collectors like Mrs. Rothkin's grandkid, here."

Andrea had a brief flash of being grateful that Madison's secret was still a secret.

"People will pay top-dollar if they think they're getting something better than what someone else has," he snorted. "They never even ask for proof."

After watching Madison shop, Andrea agreed.

"So Steve would bring you the forgeries and you'd, what? Hold on to them? Deliver them to buyers?"

"Pfft," he scoffed. "Jackman thought he was running the show. He had the forgers, but no place to sell them. The people who came into his gallery weren't the 'gardens and flowers' type, you know?"

That's it. It all came together: *Mike* was the one moving the paintings, sure, but he was also finding the buyers. Anyone with money and taste docked their boats at Beach Hill. He kept the forgery business going.

"And you connected them. And… what? Someone found out their supposedly stolen painting was a fake?"

Mike's face turned brick red. Andrea'd hit a nerve. She pushed harder.

"So the night of the murder, you and Steve and… someone else were on that boat to discuss things, huh? And there was an argument and one of you killed him?" As the words left her mouth, Andrea realized that figuring out the truth was probably the worst thing she could do right now. She clamped her lips closed. Mike stalked around the island, scowling.

"Steve paid the guy off, and he left. But Jackman wanted to shut the whole operation down. I couldn't have that."

All of this info was super-great, of course, but Andrea was still taped to her seat. And being taped to a chair typically had only one outcome:. And in movies it was not good.

"Gotcha. Well, this has been great. You heading out of town?" Andrea really hoped Capt. Mike would just saunter off and leave her here. The worst she'd have to worry about would be having to pee before she was discovered.

He pointed his finger at her in a comically villainous way. "*You're* the one heading out! Once you get the old heave-ho off the cliff, no one's going to find you and I'll be long gone by the time anyone comes looking."

Andrea's stomach did its own heave-ho, with a giant lurch. Captain Mike meant what he said.

CHAPTER 27

"So you're just going to… what? Throw me off the cliff? Really?" Andrea said. Captain Mike moved behind her chair, fiddling with the tape at her wrists.

Her heart slammed in her chest as panic hit. Her body screamed, *"get away! Get away!"* The urge to run overwhelmed her, but her ankles were still taped to the chair legs. His hot breath tickled her neck.

"That's right."

A tug against her shoulders. Mike had cut the tape binding her wrists to the back of the chair free. Her wrists were still stuck together, but she had more range of motion.

Capt. Mike leaned around the chair, showing her a pointy, well-used box cutter. "Don't try anything funny," he said.

Adrenaline sizzled in her veins, but she managed a nod. *Sure, I'm just going to let you walk me across the kitchen, out the door, and throw me off a cliff,* she thought.

And then it hit her like ice water: There *was* a way she could save her life. She had to be careful—

One ankle cut free

And not act too soon—

The other ankle free.

"Get up," Mike growled. He clutched her upper arm,

squeezing so hard she knew she'd have bruises later, and pulled her to her feet. She wobbled for a minute, the adrenaline making her lightheaded. He pulled her along anyway, and she stumbled while trying to keep her legs under her.

Get it together, girl. You've got one chance, she told herself.

Just as she'd hoped, he hustled her straight to the French door in the breakfast nook—the one that stuck so terribly.

Andrea took a deep breath as Captain Mike reached for the door with his right arm. Impossibly, he tightened the squeeze on her biceps with his left hand. She winced. The door stuck.

He leaned a little to put more pressure on it.

It was time. Andrea bent at the waist, and as fast and hard as she could, snapped her head back and to the side like she was wrapping her hair in a towel after a shower—a hopefully life-saving snap.

The side of her head, above and just behind her right ear, connected with Captain Mike's nose with an audible *crunch!* He howled and released her arm.

Go-go-go!

She spun, a little wobbly since her hands were still taped behind her, and raced across the kitchen, past the sitting room, and into the foyer. She headed straight for the front door—and the alarm panel right next to it.

From the kitchen came an expletive and a crash as a bar stool fell over. Andrea bent her knees and aimed her nose right at the red PANIC button on the alarm panel. Smooshed her nose into the red square. Hoped for lights and sirens and help to fall from the sky, but the button flashed once and went back to its regular dull silicone red. Should she hit it a second time?

"I'm going to kill you, you—"

She didn't wait to hear what he was calling her. Straightening and taking off again, Andrea raced toward the far side of the house, opposite the kitchen.

This was the part that was still under construction. With her shoulder, she pushed against the plastic sheet that separated the wing under renovation from the main rooms of the house.

Hardwood gave way to brown paper taped down to protect the floors. Her footsteps echoed. She ducked into the second room on the right, spun, and closed the door behind her.

A gutted room. Was it going to be a bathroom? A closet? Something else? She didn't care, as long as the door locked.

Luckily, it did. And it was a push button lock, thank goodness!

Finally, something going my way, she thought as she spun around and groped for the knob. She managed to push the lock in.

Just in time, too, because the rustle of the plastic floated through the door and she heard it over her ragged breathing. Captain Mike was in the hallway!

With her back to the door, Andrea scanned the room to see if there was anything that would help her get her hands free: A hammer, a pile of nails, some pieces of wood, and a lot of sawdust. The window overlooked the backyard, but it opened at the top and Andrea immediately realized it was too small to climb through.

BAM! Captain Mike threw himself against the door.

There was a nail sticking out from one of the two by fours in the wall. She had to stand on tiptoe, but between that and some uncomfortable shoulder stretching, she got the edge of the tape above the nail.

BAM! Again. The door shook, but held. Andrea was grateful that Madison didn't cut corners and get hollow doors.

One time, in a movie, she'd seen a heroine escape this way: holding her wrists as far apart as the tape would allow, then slamming with her body weight onto the protrusion so the nail broke right through the tape.

She licked her lips. *Movies do not always reflect reality. BAM!*

She held her wrists apart and drove herself down onto the nail.

The tape separated, and so did the skin on her left wrist as the nail's head scraped against her. She did it again, wincing at the sting, blood running down her hand. Then she pulled her arms apart as hard as she could.

The tape tore.

Shoulders aching, hand bloody, arms free, she picked up the hammer and faced the door.

CHAPTER 28

B*AM!* Captain Mike threw himself against the door for a third time.

This time, the wood started to give.

"I'm coming in there!" he bellowed.

Andrea readied herself with the hammer. Should she throw it? Hang on and swing at his head? To use a hammer you had to get awfully close...

The next *BAM*! didn't come. It was eerily quiet on the other side of the door. Except... was that...? Sirens?

Sirens!

Andrea let out a ragged breath of relief. The sound grew closer, and hope continued to rise.

And the hallway stayed quiet. Andrea figured that Capt. Mike must have fled when he heard the sounds, too, rather than get trapped in Madison's driveway.

Her hands shook and her knees felt like jelly. She leaned against one of the partially constructed walls, trying to catch her breath. Her injured hand throbbed. Blood dripped down her wrist, to her sleeve.

I'll need a tetanus shot for sure, she thought.

But imagining a painful needle stick suddenly gave her a rush of gratitude for being alive to get it.

She hoped she would be alive to get it.

There was a muffled thumping from another part of the house. Had the police arrived, or was it a trick? Andrea waited.

"Andrea Biscotti!" came Niles Needermeyer's voice. She'd never been so happy to hear that nasally whine, or her name pronounced incorrectly. "This is the police! Please show yourself if you're here and able!"

She threw open the door.

"I'm here!" she called. "I'm right here."

EPILOGUE

"We could not have asked for a better day," Didi said, passing around a tray of lemon-raspberry cupcakes. "Look at this!"

The sun glittered over the water, which was as smooth as the cove could get.

Andrea agreed, then took a cupcake with her non-bandaged hand. The injured one still throbbed—she hadn't needed stitches, thankfully—but was bandaged and awkward. And she didn't want to get any cupcake icing on the gauze.

"I've never had this view of the parade before," she said lightly. Madison had rented a schooner for the weekend and parked it off the coast, in the cove, facing Beach Hill.

Didi, Boo, AJ, Gwennie, Ricky, and Jack had all received invitations to watch the parade from the boat. Di and Boo, although reluctant to close the tea shoppe on such a busy day, settled on offering breakfast bundles of pastries and other delights for patrons to order in advance and pick up early in the morning.

The parade boats were behind the Point, out of view.

From her perch on the deck cushion, Andrea could see all of Beach Hill stretching along the water. Picnickers filled Front Street Park, people lined the beach on the Point, and there were colorful banners and balloons tied to the lampposts.

"Nice hat," Ricky said, his mouth full of cupcake.

Andrea grinned and adjusted the torn brim. "Thanks. I'm a Sea Dogs fan now," she joked.

AJ finished his cupcake and put his arm around her. "Feeling okay?"

She nodded. For the first couple of days after being trapped in Madison's house, she'd had nightmares. They seemed over now.

"I'm just so glad they caught him."

Captain Mike had been captured in Connecticut, close to the gallery, taken into custody, and confessed everything: He and Jackman had run a good-sized forgery ring, with buyers coming in to Beach Hill and Mike moving the paintings and collecting the cash. The night of the murder, an angry buyer realized the art he thought was stolen was actually a forgery. He threatened to blow the operation open, and blackmailed Jackman. Mike, Jackman, and the buyer met on the Master Peace. Jackman had brought the duffel of cash and had paid the buyer off, with some left for Mike to close out the operation. After the buyer left, Jackman and Mike argued, with Mike ending the discussion with a wrench to Steve's head and a shove overboard. He hadn't realized Ratchet Bob and Ricky were there doing work on the engine until Ratchet Bob came up. He left with Bob, accidentally grabbing the bag that contained Ricky's party clothes.

Then Ricky came up and saw the blood on the wrench. He peered over the side of the boat to see if he could see Steve, lost his hat, and fled, grabbing the bag that contained the money. He tried to give it back to Mike that night, but got thwarted because he sent the text to Gwennie. When Mike realized he had the wrong bag, he threatened to hurt Gwen if Ricky didn't play along with the police.

And in the meantime, he took care of the loose end of the

buyer, who owned The Lazy Sunday. The man had been strangled and left on his boat.

Andrea shuddered, remembering how effortlessly Mike tied the knots in the sail cord when she was in the Shore Shack. She hadn't had all the pieces, but she'd had enough to let Mike know she was a threat. He had every intention of throwing her off that cliff.

"And I'm so glad my tech worked." The panic button not only alerted the police, but AJ. And he knew that if Andrea had hit it, something had to be very wrong. So he followed up the alert with a phone call.

"Look!" Madison squealed. "It's starting!"

The first boat emerged from behind the Point. Bedecked in bright flags and bearing a huge inflatable lobster on its bow, it cruised into the cove.

"Are they all like that?"

Jack chuckled. "Each owner can decorate their boat however they want. You'll see some good ones."

"If it weren't for you, I wouldn't be seeing any of this ," Ricky said, nudging Andrea with his knee.

"And I'd need to pay extra for cottage maintenance," Andrea teased. She was so happy that he was back—personality and all.

"'If it weren't for you,' seems to be the new catchphrase around Andrea," Madison said. "If it weren't for you, I wouldn't have moved to Beach Hill. Or met Jack."

"If it weren't for you, I wouldn't have my brother back," Gwennie said.

Andrea flushed.

More boats emerged, each more colorful and quirky than the last. The breeze picked up, rocking the boat gently.

"And if it weren't for you all, Beach Hill wouldn't be home," Andrea said.

THE END

ACKNOWLEDGMENTS

It takes a village to make a book:

Thanks to my Table for 7 team: Gary, Phoebe, Megan, and Wendy for their support, critique, and enthusiasm for this project. You make my writing better. Most amazing writing group ever!

To the real-life Di and Boo: I'm so grateful you're my friends.

To Steve Leavey: Thank you for the realtor expertise!

I'm grateful to Heather Kelly and Kristen Wixted for their support and guidance in this indie author world.

A big thanks to Nancy Werlin and Toni Buzzeo, for their help in sorting out crimes and plot lines. I am forever grateful.

Thank you to Natasha Sass, for welcoming me into and guiding me through the cozy mystery world.

A bunch of gratitude to Donna at DLR Cover Designs, who made this book beautiful.

To Kathy Vines, for keeping me on track and focused during this whole process. Thank you so much!

And a big, heartfelt thank you to Frank, who helped me come up with Andrea during our pandemic walks, and believed I could tell these stories. I love you so much.

ABOUT THE AUTHOR

Mina Allan writes cozy mysteries and plots fictional dastardly deeds from her home in Massachusetts. She likes seaside views, fruity cocktails, and is always in search of the perfect purse. Find her online at www.minaallan.com.

instagram.com/mina.allan.books

ALSO BY MINA ALLAN

Available now

A Precarious Perch: A Beach Hill Cozy Short Story

The story of how Madison and Andrea meet.

Coming in 2023

A Midwinter's Mix-Up:

A Beach Hill Cozy Short Story

Chowder & Chicanery:

A Beach Hill Cozy Mystery

Book 2